Tess

I dismount, careful not to let Granddad see how grateful I am to feel steady ground beneath my feet. Tess mouths the bit. She throws her head, tossing froth on me. Bloodstained froth. The bit has rubbed her poor mouth raw.

I give Granddad what I believe is a bright smile and say, "Well, what do you think?"

"She's a handful, Willojean."

"Yessir."

"But you're a handful, too." Granddad studies Tess. He studies me. "Can you control her?"

"I think so."

"Think so? Or know so?" Granddad gives me the admiral's stare.

I don't flinch. "Know so."

✖✖✖

"Has much to offer beyond the standard equine love story themes. . . . Keehn quietly delivers a powerful emotional punch through empathic characterizations and a deceptively simple story line . . . [and] movingly illustrates the redemptive power of love, as well as the importance of letting go when love just isn't enough."   —*Publishers Weekly*

"A typical girl-and-her-horse story is transformed by Keehn into a novel about pain, loss, love, forgiveness, and redemption."   —*Kirkus Reviews*

OTHER PUFFIN BOOKS YOU MAY ENJOY

THE FIRST HORSE I SEE

Sally M. Keehn

PUFFIN BOOKS

PUFFIN BOOKS
Published by the Penguin Group
Penguin Putnam Books for Young Readers,
345 Hudson Street, New York, New York 10014, U.S.A.
Penguin Books Ltd, 27 Wrights Lane, London W8 5TZ, England
Penguin Books Australia Ltd, Ringwood, Victoria, Australia
Penguin Books Canada Ltd, 10 Alcorn Avenue, Toronto, Ontario, Canada M4V 3B2
Penguin Books (N.Z.) Ltd, 182-190 Wairau Road, Auckland 10, New Zealand

Penguin Books Ltd, Registered Offices: Harmondsworth, Middlesex, England

First published in the United States of America by Philomel Books,
a division of Penguin Putnam Books for Young Readers, 1999
Published by Puffin Books,
a division of Penguin Putnam Books for Young Readers, 2000

7 9 10 8 6

THE LIBRARY OF CONGRESS HAS CATALOGED THE PHILOMEL EDITION AS FOLLOWS:
Keehn, Sally M. The first horse I see / Sally M. Keehn.
p. cm.
Summary: Left in the care of her beloved Granddad following the death of her
mother, Willojean tries to prove to her alcoholic father that she is able to
train a special horse which had been abused.
I. Title. PZ7.K2257 Wi 1999 [Fic]—dc21 98-15706 CIP AC
ISBN 0-399-23351-2

This edition ISBN 0-698-11867-7

Printed in the United States of America

For my brothers—Bob, Jim and John Miller—
who knew and loved Mas-Que

THE FIRST HORSE I SEE

CHAPTER
1

The bay mare stands alone beneath an oak tree that provides the only shade in a horse dealer's muddy paddock. I can tell right off that she's been badly treated—starved so thin I can count her ribs. Fresh barbed-wire cuts cross her flanks and dried manure stains her reddish-brown coat. Eyes closed, head hung low, she rests while flies feed off saddle sores festering on her withers. My first thought is, whoever owned this horse should be sent to prison forever and ever. My second is, I want to take her home.

She raises her head as Granddad, the dealer and I approach. She has a beautiful face with shiny dark eyes that surprise me, for I had thought they'd be dulled by pain. Her eyes reflect not only the light of the steamy-hot June morning, but also me—a thin line of blond, white shirt and jeans.

"Her racing name is Grassmere's Contessa," the dealer says. "We call her Tess."

Tess. I like that name.

"She's a registered Thoroughbred." The dealer grabs Tess's upper lip and curls it inside out to show Granddad and me the black letters and numbers tattooed there. She struggles to get away from him, but he keeps holding on. When he finally releases her, she snorts at him.

I smile to myself and rub my hand along the stripe that runs from a star between her eyes to her soft gray muzzle. She butts her head against my chest.

"She's an eight-year-old. Been off the racetrack about four years," the dealer says. "Ex-racehorses make the best show hunters. You did say you wanted a show hunter?"

"One that jumps," I say, and Granddad says, "That's right." He runs his hands down Tess's legs to check them for splints and wind-puffs—calcium deposits along her cannon bones and fetlock joints—that can lame her. Although Granddad is a retired Navy admiral and spent thirty years working with aircraft carriers, he grew up with horses. He knows them almost as well as he knows ships.

Tess doesn't seem to mind Granddad's examining her legs, but when he straightens up and the fine white hair on his head brushes a scratch along her belly, her ears flatten: *Don't touch me there.*

"She's had a tough life." Granddad gives the dealer what I call "the admiral's stare," sharp and questioning.

"A hot-tempered cowboy owned her," the dealer explains. "He tried to turn her into a barrel racer. He beat her up a bit."

I wish for the cowboy what Granddad wishes for all the cruel people of this world—that they be hung from the yardarms of a ship. And let the seagulls pick their flesh.

"She's a good horse," the dealer says. "All she needs is to get into the right hands and she'll thrive." He looks at me.

I am petting Tess's neck. I feel tiny bumps where dirt and sweat have inflamed her skin. *I'd give you a decent home. I'd never hurt you.* Tess reaches around to nuzzle my pocket. I give her a carrot and she gives me her breath, warm against my palm.

"Want to ride her?" the dealer says. "You do know how to ride."

"Yessir." I've had two years of lessons. The first year

was when we lived in California. The second, after we'd moved here to Maryland. I've taken my Maryland lessons from Diana Wolf, who's the best riding instructor in the world. What would she think of my buying an abused horse? Would she think that I could heal it? I'm painting Diana's paddock this afternoon. I'll ask.

The dealer hurries off to get Tess's tack. His boots splash through filmy puddles. There's no grass in sight. His stable is nothing but stalls and a tack room strung together along one side of the sagging barbed-wire paddock. I want to get Tess out of here.

Granddad, who knows me almost as well as I know myself, says in a low voice, "Willojean, what did I tell you on the car ride over?"

"To buy a horse with fire in its eyes. A horse with spirit," I say.

"What else?"

"Not to fall in love with the first horse I see. But Granddad, this first horse needs me. And she's a Thoroughbred! She likes me."

"Any horse would like you." Granddad ruffles my hair. "We have all summer to find the right one."

"This *feels* like the right one." Tess nuzzles me again. I give her my last carrot and wish I'd brought a thousand more. "Mom said I could have any horse I wanted."

"Your father's the commanding officer now," Granddad says softly.

"He doesn't know horses. He couldn't tell a good one from a bad one. Besides, he's never home. He told us we could pick mine out."

"He said any horse within reason."

"Tess is within reason."

Granddad sighs. "If you're serious about buying Tess, a vet will need to check her out. But don't pin your hopes on her, Willo. She's in bad shape."

I want to pin my hopes on her.

The dealer returns, carrying an old beat-up English saddle and a western bridle with a curb bit. It has long shanks, a high port and a chain. It hurts me to watch the dealer force that bit into Tess's mouth. When he draws the crownpiece over Tess's ears, the bit pulls up against her lips. She throws her head.

"That bridle's too small," I say.

"It's the only one I have right now." He glances at me. "You did say you wanted to ride."

"Yessir." If I don't ride Tess, there's no way Granddad will let me buy her.

The saddle's stirrup leathers are old. They've been broken off and can't be lengthened enough for my long legs. Mounted on Tess with my feet propped in the stirrups, I am like a grasshopper—my knees are up to my chin and my rear hangs over the cantle. I'm glad Dad's far away in California. I wouldn't want him to see this. Granddad just says, "You and Tess make quite a pair."

As soon as the dealer releases Tess, she takes off at a trot. This surprises me because I thought we'd walk first. Her springy trot is hard to post to. It takes several times around the paddock to get used to it. Just as I start to get comfortable, Granddad calls, "Try her at a walk."

I don't want to hurt Tess's mouth, so I pull gently on the reins. She throws her head and keeps on trotting. I pull again. She trots on. I take a deep breath, grip the reins and pull sharply, hoping she'll come to a gradual walk—the way Sweets, Diana's easygoing chestnut mare, always has. Tess stops dead and I almost keep on going.

"That bit stops her on a dime." The dealer chuckles. I don't think it's funny. Tess starts to back up. I urge her forward. She tosses her head and backs up more. The dealer yells, "Stop pulling on those reins!"

Was I? I loosen my grip and Tess stops in front of the manure pile. I want to dismount—even though I haven't cantered. Tess needs a gentler bit for that. I need a better saddle.

But Granddad, who loves to play poker, has always told me, "Never give up because of the hand you've been dealt. Play it the best way you can." And so, when the dealer says, "Try her at a canter," I take a deep breath and I try.

All I do is nudge Tess with my outside leg and she plunges forward. I grab her mane to keep from falling off. We race by Granddad, his sea-blue eyes widening in surprise. We race past the stable. Thank goodness the paddock is small. It keeps us in a circle that Tess rounds like a supercharged carousel horse with me, the grasshopper, perched on top.

"Sit back, Willo," Granddad orders. "And for God's sake, talk to her."

I sit back. I flop all over. I mutter to Tess, "If you'd only behave, I'd take you to Granddad's farm. Instead of a paddock with a single tree, it has a hundred and fifty acres of woods and fields you can explore."

Tess flicks her ears. "Granddad's farm has meadows filled with grass," I say. She slows a little. "There's Maiden Creek for swimming. And the barn. It's a big red barn with big box stalls and Toby. He's my friend Dove's fat brown pony. You'd love Toby."

Tess gallops, I talk about the farm, the dealer leaves to answer a phone and Granddad says, "All right. Bring her to a walk."

This time I prepare myself by bracing my feet against the stirrups. I pull back sharply. Tess gallops a few more strides, ducks her head, gives a little buck, and then, finally, she stops.

I dismount, careful not to let Granddad see how grateful I am to feel steady ground beneath my feet. Tess mouths the bit. She throws her head, tossing froth on me. Bloodstained froth. The bit has rubbed her poor mouth raw.

I give Granddad what I believe is a bright smile and say, "Well, what do you think?"

"She's a handful, Willojean."

"Yessir."

"But you're a handful, too." Granddad studies Tess. He studies me. "Can you control her?"

"I think so."

"Think so? Or know so?" Granddad gives me the admiral's stare. I don't flinch. "Know so."

"She'll need to pass the vet's inspection," he warns. "Your father's as well."

"I know, Granddad."

"Then I'll tell you what I think. She's thin, flea-bitten and battle-scarred. But she's got a powerful way of moving that raises the hair along my neck. And by God, Willojean, the mare's got spirit."

CHAPTER 2

Wherever Granddad happened to be stationed, whether it was England, Italy or the Philippines, he'd get people together to play poker. Twenty years ago, at his last duty station near Washington, D.C., he mentioned to some poker buddies that he was planning to retire and buy Colonel Winters's farm, which was about twenty miles away in Maryland.

"I know that farm," one of his buddies said. "You'd be crazy to buy it. The house is full of dry rot—the barn's falling down."

"The whole place needs work," another said.

"Nothing wrong with a little work," my granddad

said. He squinted at five poker cards he'd just been dealt, all facedown on the table. "Let's see what the cards say."

He turned the cards over one by one, and all together they said royal flush. In poker, you can't do better than that. The next day he bid on Colonel Winters's farm and got it. He named it "Mas-Que," which, according to Granddad, is pidgin English for *Oh, what the heck.*

Dad says all Granddad really needed to buy Mas-Que was for someone to tell him he'd be crazy to do it. Dad designs spy planes for a living. They're so crazy-looking no one thinks they'll fly, but they do. Dad and Granddad get along just fine.

Granddad's big white farmhouse with its green shutters and red chimney stands at the end of a mile-long dirt road on Mas-Que's highest spot—a hilly bank overlooking Maiden Creek. Granddad says it's always wise to have your house built high. That way you can keep an eye on the troops. By the time I'd moved to Mas-Que, Granddad had developed heart trouble and so his troops of cows, pigs, sheep and chickens had dwindled. However, he still had his first lieutenant—an orange cat named Sir Alexander Boswell.

It's noon when Granddad and I return from the horse dealer's, and I find Boswell sleeping on a pile of

Dad's white underwear. Josefa, my best friend Dove's grandmother who helps us with housework on Monday mornings, has folded this underwear and piled it neatly on Dad's bed because he doesn't like anyone putting things away in his drawers. He'll take care of that himself, thank you.

I plop a sleepy Boswell on the floor. He watches me shake his hair off a pair of Dad's underpants and fold them back as best I can. "Everything must be perfect when Dad gets home," I explain. "That way, he'll be in a happy mood for meeting Tess. He has to like her! Oh, I hope the vet says she's okay."

I neatly pile the mail I've just brought upstairs on the far left corner of Dad's green desk blotter. By Friday, when he returns from California where he's been working for the Navy on the A-22 Stealth Intruder, five piles of mail will be lined up on his blotter like sailors ready for inspection.

Draping a purring Boswell around my neck, I carry him across the hall to my room. I plop him on my bed, which is high off the floor, with a horsehair mattress that belonged to my Great-grandmother Elsie. When I lie on it, I can see out the window to the barn, downhill and nestled among trees. For the past two weeks, I've cleaned out old cow manure and cobwebs from that barn. I've got a box stall ready for a horse like Tess.

"A horse. A horse. My kingdom for a horse," I chant as I throw on old clothes to paint Diana's fences.

The phone rings. I pick up the upstairs one just as Granddad picks up the downstairs one. A man says to Granddad, "I got your message. I have an hour free this afternoon. I'll check out that mare for you."

The veterinarian.

Heart pounding, I put the phone back down. "Tess is going to be just fine," I say aloud in my mother's voice, low-pitched and certain. Mom knew all about horses. She had one wherever she and Granddad happened to live. Mom would have liked Tess, with her proud spirit and way of moving that raises the hair along Granddad's neck.

I wish Mom were here. But she's not and she never will be anymore. Dad says we must all try hard and get used to it. I hope he's trying as hard as I am.

I race downstairs. At the step before the landing where a white door leads off into Granddad's office, I grab the balled end of the banister post. Pivoting off my left hand, I fly through the air, turning, reaching with my feet for the living room floor. If I make it, everything will be all right. Dad will be happy. I'll be—

I clear the landing, but for the millionth time this year, crash on the step leading up to it.

"Willojean!" Granddad shouts from the kitchen.

"I'm okay." Rubbing my head, I get slowly to my

feet. One day I'll jump well enough to clear that land-ing and the step besides. I will!

In the kitchen, Granddad hands me a fried cheese and bacon sandwich, all wrapped up in a paper towel because he knows I must be off and running.

"If the vet phones about Tess—"

"I'll call you at Diana's. But Willo . . ."

"I know. I'm not to pin my hopes on this one," I say as I head out the door.

At the dock, I untie Granddad's big old clunky rowboat, *The Admiral.* I climb into the middle seat, settle the heavy oars into their locks and row toward a broken-down dock that belongs to an abandoned summer cottage. From there, it's a ten-minute hike down a dirt road and across Ferry Highway to Diana's. I know the route by heart. I've taken it a million times.

I row past Dad's sleek and silent sailboat, the *Bon-nie Prince Charlie,* which is moored in deep water off Granddad's dock. The twenty-two-foot sloop, painted green with a small cabin that sleeps two, hasn't left its mooring since last November.

The tide is low. The air is still and settles over me like a hot wet blanket smelling of seaweed and dead fish. The few houses I see along the shore have their shades drawn against the heat. There's no one on the creek but me. I'm so worried about Tess. To calm my-self, to keep myself company as I row I sing my version of Buckeye Jim, which Mom and I always sang when she'd drive me to my riding lessons:

> *Way up yonder above the sky,*
> *A bay mare pranced in a blue jay's eye.*
> *Buckeye Jim, you can't go,*
> *Go weave and spin, you can't go,*
> *Buckeye Jim.*

CHAPTER
3

Diana's farm is smaller than Granddad's—thirty acres instead of a hundred and fifty. Her farm is only four years old. Almost everything is painted white—the fences, the cinder-block stable, the big two-story house with its wide front porch and five pillars.

But it has secret places that aren't white. There's a dark corner in Diana's feed room where she pushed aside corn and showed me baby mice, small and pink, all asleep in a soft gray nest. And there's her bathroom. Diana has her own bathroom with peach-flowered wallpaper and gold faucets. Perfume, nail polish, hair spray, lipstick—all kinds of things are spread out on her vanity. Beneath it, stored inside, are sanitary napkins—whenever I should need them.

I needed them last month when I got my period for the first time. I was riding Sweets. I was a mess and so embarrassed. "Don't be," Diana said. "Getting your period is as natural as breathing." I love Diana. She makes embarrassing things unembarrassing; she faces them—chin up and shoulders squared.

The air I'm breathing now is hot and sticky and smells of horse manure and wet paint. Colin, Diana's fourteen-year-old son, is painting the paddock along with Dove and me. The paddock leads off from the cinder-block stable, all white except for some black trim. Heads hanging over their stall doors, Sweets and Cloudy, Colin's gray gelding, watch us with eyes half closed against the heat.

"Have you ever seen a horse for the first time and just known it was right for you?" I ask. I've been telling Dove and Colin about Tess ever since I arrived twenty minutes earlier.

"No." Colin slaps paint on a post while I whiten the outside top rail leading into it. The closer I get to him, the warmer I feel. I'd like to melt into his heart.

"The first time I saw Toby, I knew that sweet fat pony was right for me," Dove says. She paints the inside of the bottom rail and we both are nearing Colin.

"Toby will never make a jumper," Colin says.

"Why not?" Dove asks, her paintbrush poised.

"He's too fat. All he cares about is eating."

"So. I'll bribe him to jump. With food." Dove reaches over and with her brush dabs a white spot on the tip of Colin's nose. I'd never dare do that, but Dove can because she and Colin are close friends. "Just friends," she once told me. "I'd never dream of kissing him."

I would.

Colin has red hair, and with his white nose he looks like a clown. I giggle, but Colin doesn't react. Something over Dove's left shoulder has caught his attention.

Uphill from us, Colin's stepdad, Jack, carries golf clubs over to a white pickup that's parked alongside Diana's ring. Jack has thick curly blond hair and the kind of face that's red, summer and winter. According to Colin, Jack's the one who wants everything painted white. Colin claims it's Jack's cover-up—to hide the blackness of his heart.

Jack dumps his clubs into the truck bed. He wipes his face with a handkerchief and opens the cab door. He climbs inside, where he starts fiddling with something I can't see.

Colin turns back to Dove. His face looks serious, white nose and all. He resumes talking as if Jack's presence hasn't interrupted him. "You can never bribe a horse. He has to want to jump. In here." He touches the tip of his brush against Dove's faded green T-shirt. It leaves a tiny spot just about where her heart beats.

"Can you bribe a vet into saying a horse is sound?" I say. "The vet has got to say that Tess is sound."

"People can be bribed." Colin's hazel eyes, as steamy to me as the afternoon, gaze into mine.

"The vet's probably examining Tess right now," I tell Colin's eyes. "He's probably feeling lumps Grand-dad didn't find. What if Tess has heart problems? Or worms?"

"Stop it, Willo." Dove grabs my arms and shakes me.

I look at Dove's green eyes and say, "I don't care if Tess has lumps. I'll buy her anyway. If Dad doesn't like it, I'll just—" I pause. What will I do? Dad *is* the commanding officer now.

"Stop worrying," Dove says. "You worry too much." She turns to Colin. "Hold Willo for me."

Colin, without hesitating or asking why, grabs my arms and pins them to my sides. I should struggle. I should try to get away. But Colin's breath smells of peppermint gum. A lock of hair has fallen into his face.

Dove dabs a paint-wet finger against my forehead. She rubs her finger round and round. Her hair, wild and brown and curly, frames her tan face like a halo. "This is a holy circle I am painting," she says. "It has no beginning. It has no end. It circles on and on, taking away all worries and bringing nothing but peace and good fortune into your life."

"Really?"

Dove, wide-eyed, nods. She's part Mexican, Italian and Irish, and she's Catholic. She goes to Masses where a priest burns incense and people pray and finger beads, so I believe her.

"You silly clowns. I'm paying you to paint the paddock, not each other," a voice behind us says. Diana! She was off riding when I arrived and now she's here! She's ridden up on Sultan—a big dark horse she bought last fall. He's beautiful and so is she. Diana reins him in and smiles down at us with her warm brown eyes.

Colin's face turns red. He pushes me away, rubs the paint off his nose and grabs his brush. A restless Sultan tosses his head. He was a handful when Diana first bought him and he still is. Yet, deep inside, he's a pussycat. I know. I've seen him when he's loose in the field with Sweets and Cloudy. He always lets them drink before he does. With his teeth, he scratches Sweets's back. I like how Sultan can be strong and yet gentle, too. I bet Tess will be just like that.

"I found a horse!" I tell Diana.

"So soon?" she says.

"It was the first horse I saw. A bay mare. A Thoroughbred. I think she'll make a jumper. Will you teach me how to teach her?" The words come tumbling out of me.

"Of course," Diana says. Sultan wheels. Over her shoulder she continues, "When you get her, call me. We'll set up some lessons." She's wearing red nail polish, the exact color of a bow she's tied to a flowing lock in Sultan's mane.

"I like his bow!" I call as he carries her away.

"It's to remind this crazy guy he's mine." Her voice softened when she said "crazy guy." She really loves Sultan. He's a deep dark brown—the color of Maiden Creek at night. He moves so smoothly. He seems to flow like water, his muscles rippling as he prances away from us and up to the hilltop ring where, for the past year, both Dove and I have taken lessons.

Proudly, he carries his tail high. He passes some red-and-white barrels and trots toward Jack's truck, which is parked alongside the opposite side of the fence. Jack's still there? Why? He stares out the windshield at the approaching horse. When Sultan's about a nose-length away from the truck, the engine, which has stood idle all this time, sputters to life.

Sultan halts. Wild-eyed, he starts backing up. The truck sputters and smokes. Jack guns the accelerator and the engine roars. Sultan rears.

"Oh my goodness," Dove whispers.

Sultan dances on his hind legs—a huge dark horse spread out between the earth and sky. Jack's pickup lurches forward. It turns, moving slowing away from the ring. Sultan comes down on his forelegs. He bolts with Diana, his hooves churning up a sea of dust.

"The jerk!" Colin says. "If Sultan had fallen backward . . ."

"Jack didn't realize what he was doing," Dove says.

"You don't know him the way I do," Colin says. "He's psycho. As soon as Mom married him he turned psycho. He's a creep."

I wish Colin wouldn't say this. If Diana hadn't married Jack, she and Colin would never have moved here from Massachusetts and I never would have met them. I'd never have had Diana teach me.

It's not until Jack's pickup turns onto the macadam road leading to the highway that Diana regains control of Sultan. She slows him to a canter. Now a flowing trot.

"She's all right. They're both all right," I say.

We watch her circle him several times and then bring him to a walk. Then we go back to painting. We talk about rock groups, horse shows, veterinarians and a Catholic retreat Dove went on where she learned about French kissing—it's a sin. We don't mention Jack. Did he mean to frighten Sultan? I don't know and I don't think I want to know.

It's the end of June. Corn planted in an adjacent farmer's field stands knee-high. Uphill, in the ring, Diana gallops Sultan past the bright green corn and toward a four-foot post and rail. He approaches the fence squarely, facing it head-on. Diana rises over his lathered neck. A stride away, he lifts beneath her and his powerful hindquarters propel them both off the ground and into the air. For a moment, they're suspended above the fence. Around them, the summer sky seems to stretch forever.

I want Tess and me to be like that. I want us to jump fences, barrels, gates, chicken coops. . . . Diana could teach us how. Oh, I hope the vet says Tess is sound. He just has to!

CHAPTER 4

"The vet called—he's seen her," Granddad says as soon as I come into the kitchen. The screen door slams behind me and a fan set on top of the radiator blows the smell of the onions Granddad's frying into my face.

"What did he say? Is Tess all right? Can I buy her?"

Granddad puts down his spatula. With the edge of his Big Chef's apron, he wipes sweat off his forehead and says, "Well, her legs are sound. Her heartbeat's strong and her lungs are clear."

"Yes!" I dance across the black-and-tan-tiled kitchen floor while Boswell eyes me from his command post—the top of the refrigerator.

"She has a low fever, Willo." Granddad's words stop me midstep.

"What does that mean?"

"Infection. Dr. Beidleman isn't sure from what. Maybe the saddle sores. He's given her antibiotics. He says we should wait a few days. See if they work."

"But I want to bring her here. Now."

"Not with a fever."

"But if the fever goes away, I can get her?" I wanted to make this a statement, but it comes out as a question. It hangs in the hot kitchen like a dead fly in a spider's web.

Granddad examines that fly from eyeballs to wing tips. "The mare has worms. Her teeth need filing—"

"I'll pay for the worm medicine. I'll pay the dentist." I dig into my jeans pocket and bring out the twenty dollars I've earned from painting the paddock.

"There's more to this than money," Granddad says. "Even if Tess gets over the fever, she'll need new shoes, vitamins, eight quarts of grain a day, several days of rest before you can even think of riding her—"

"I can handle this."

"Are you sure?"

"Of course I'm sure! I can handle anything."

Except for the heat. I can't handle the heat. At dinner, I'm so hot I kick off my sneakers to let the kitchen floor cool my feet. The rotating fan blows sticky hair out of my face. But it can't reach my stomach, where Granddad's spicy bean and hamburger casserole wars with a worry that's just occurred to me. To shake a fever, Tess needs to be kept cool. But how? The dealer has one scraggly tree for shade.

"When I get a high fever, my Grandma Josefa puts me in a bathtub of warm water," Dove tells me the next day at the barn. "Little by little, she adds cold water to the bath. Before you know it, bingo, my fever's down and I'm practically all well."

"There's no bathtub at the horse dealer's," I say.

"Good point." Dove unsaddles Toby. It's nine A.M. and she's just taken him on an early-morning ride. Toby's covered in sweat from the heat and his belly's heaving. I walk alongside Dove as she cools him down.

Next to the barnyard, ten rows of a hundred Scotch pines each—that's a thousand little Christmas trees—look on. They remind me of brave little sailors standing at attention in their sunbaked field that used to grow tobacco. Dove helped Dad, Granddad and me plant the trees last spring.

Once Toby's breathing calms, we sponge him off—the water steaming off his sleek plump body. And then Dove helps me to water all the little Christmas trees we can reach with the hose.

"If Tess were here, I'd water her," I say as I watch the dry ground around a tiny pine turn wet and dark. "We need a thunderstorm, Dove. With lots of wind and rain. That would cool Tess off."

The next day is even hotter. It's so hot neither Granddad nor I feel like eating breakfast. By noon, it's 105 degrees. "Tess will never get better," I tell Dove. We've been hanging around the barn, too hot and tired to do anything but watch Toby sleep.

"Let's do something cool," Dove says.

"Want to go skinny-dipping?" I ask.

Dove widens her eyes, trying to look astonished. Then she grins. She's been skinny-dipping in the creek with me a thousand times.

I lend her a bathing suit. We both wear bathing suits to the water. No one's boating on it. The creek's all still and quiet. In the water, Dove and I slip out of our suits and tie them to the dock ladder. I swim past Dad's sailboat and out into the middle of the creek. The top layer of the water is warm and covered with silt. Lower down, the water gets cooler. I dive down there, wanting to feel that coolness all over me.

And there's Dove, swimming toward me, her curly hair fanning out. She makes a funny blowfish face at me. We grab hands and come bursting out of the cool layer, through the warm one and out into the hot summer air. Silty water streams down our faces and onto our breasts. Dove's are large while mine are barely even nubs. I keep hoping they'll get bigger.

Giggling, Dove and I climb onto the dock and then, holding hands, we run off the end of it—shrieking as we hit the water. We do this over and over again. I love the feeling of airy freedom I get as I jump off the dock. I love the sting of water followed by the deep-down coolness. I wish Tess could feel this. What if I can't get her? I'll just die!

That night—as he does every Wednesday night—Dad calls home from California. "How's everything?" he says, and I say, "Hot. It's been over a hundred degrees for the last two days." I don't tell him why I care.

"It's been a pressure cooker out here, too. I can't take any more heat. I'll be home Friday night. Late. Do a rain dance for me, Willo. Have everything cooled off."

"Yessir."

He doesn't say anything more and there's this awkward silence that I don't know how to fill. I don't mention Tess, even though she's all I think about. I wish the heat would break.

"Want to talk to Granddad? He's around here somewhere," I say.

"Not today, Willo. I have a meeting."

"Okay, Dad." There's another awkward silence, and then, we both hang up. We never seem to know what to say to each other. Mom was the one who acted as the intermediary between us. Loving Mom was what we had in common and now she's gone.

At night, it's still so hot! I'm thirsty. My sheets stick to me. I wish I could go swimming. Out the window, a full moon lights up a field where a thousand Christmas trees stand up tall—brave little sailors.

"Once you plant your trees, you be sure to water them," Mom had whispered to Granddad, Dad and me. It was in December. We'd gathered around the bed we'd set up for her in Granddad's downstairs office. Josefa, who'd been taking care of Mom, had told us she was dying. I didn't believe Josefa because moms are not allowed to die.

"Trees need so much water," Mom had said.

Hugging my pillow, I stare out the window. I wish that it would rain. I begin rocking. Back and forth. Back and forth. I hug my pillow tighter. It's so hot. Why won't it rain?

CHAPTER
5

The first time Dad saw Mom, he fell in love with her. "There was this big red horse," he says, "and your small curly-haired mom galloping him bareback along a California beach. She turned him into the ocean. I watched them hurtle over a wave and then, as a second wave crashed on shore, they disappeared from view.

"I couldn't breathe until I saw them both emerge beyond the breakers, the horse swimming beneath your mother—two fearless creatures of the sea. I knew then—*This woman is the one for me.*"

This scene that Dad's described to me a million times is what I dream of Wednesday night and into

Thursday. I dream it over and over again. All but the last time, I'm the one watching from shore. I reach out my arms to Mom and I am crying—"Come back. Please. Come back."

The last time, I'm riding the horse. I'm the one who's leaving and the horse I ride is Tess. I cling to her wet black mane. A cold wave crashes over us. For a moment, I can't breathe. When we emerge, I discover we're in Maiden Creek! It's fall and the cool dark water reflects all these beautiful red, yellow and orange leaves.

Early in the afternoon following this dream, the horse dealer finally calls and he tells Granddad, "It's amazing. Last night, the horse was delirious. This morning, her fever's gone. She's fine." He goes on to say that he can have Tess delivered to Mas-Que on Friday at 1300 Granddad's time.

Dove and I are in the kitchen fixing milk shakes when Granddad announces this. *Can water from a dream cool down a real-life horse with fever?* I grab Dove's hands. "I don't believe it! I'm finally getting a horse!" We lean back and we swing. Faster and faster. I sing out—"A horse. A kingdom for a—"

"There is one stipulation," Granddad says.

"What stipulation?" I drop Dove's hands. We both look at Granddad.

"A week's trial period. To make certain she's healthy."

"No problem," I say. "If Tess can get over a fever in a heat wave, she's healthy."

"And," Granddad says, "we need to give the commanding officer a chance to check her over."

"Yessir." I wish the C.O. were someone other than Dad. He doesn't know horses. And lately, I don't know him. "Granddad? He called last night. I didn't know if I could get Tess, so I didn't mention her."

"I see." Granddad scratches his head and gives me a funny sort of smile. "Well then." He sighs. "We'll have to let the facts speak for themselves."

It's Friday afternoon—the longest afternoon in history. Tess was supposed to have arrived over two and a half hours ago. Dove waited with me for an hour, but then she had to leave for the beach. Is Tess ever going to come? *Where is she?*

I'm watering the Christmas trees again. With my thumb, I make the water spray out as far as it can go. I want it to reach all the trees that Dove and I missed on Wednesday. Trees need so much water.

"Where is Tess?" I call over the barnyard fence to Granddad. I've asked him this about a dozen times. He's on his back beneath the tractor, fixing something with a wrench. He gives that wrench a final twist, then wiggles out.

"Maybe the driver got lost," he says.

From far away comes the sound of tires crunching on gravel. Big tires. Truck tires?

"That's got to be Tess!" I run into the barnyard and turn off the water spigot just as a truck I feared would never come rounds Granddad's house and heads downhill toward us. Its high roof scrapes against the apple trees that line the road. Small green apples bounce against the truck and set off a frantic mooing inside.

"Cows?" I say to Granddad.

"Cows!" he says. We hurry across the barnyard. The truck backfires, then shudders to a halt at the gate. A white Buick pulls in behind the truck. Dad's white Buick.

"He said he was coming home late," I say to Granddad.

"He must have taken an earlier flight." Granddad doesn't seem worried or upset. I'm not either. Not really. It's just, I feel, I don't know, a little guilty. As if I've been caught in the middle of doing something I shouldn't.

Dad gets out of the car. Hands shoved into tan suit pants, he stares at the truck. From it now comes not only mooing, but the bam-bam-bam of kicking hooves and a desperate-to-escape high whinny. Tess? The driver climbs out of the truck and slams the door.

"What's in the truck?" Dad shouts over the racket.

"I think it's the horse I found." I wince, for the truck sounds as if it's being kicked to pieces. "She sounds a little scared."

"Scared?" The driver unbolts the truck ramp. "The mare's downright crazy. It took me over an hour to load her."

He lowers the ramp and the kicking stops. I want to die when I see Tess. Sweat covers her from head to tail. She's tied to the side of the truck and she's so afraid, she trembles. Just a few ropes strung across the truck separate her from a group of cows tightly bunched in the cargo area. They look out at us and they bawl.

The driver slowly walks up the ramp. Eyeballing him, Tess half rears, yanking at her rope.

"Knock it off!" The driver slams his fist against her head. He slams it again. Before I realize what I'm doing, I'm up the ramp. I yank on his arm and scream, "Stop hitting her!"

He stares at me as if I've gone completely crazy.

"She's my horse! I'll take care of her!"

The driver looks at Granddad. Granddad nods. *Let the girl do this.* The driver raises his hands and backs away. He heads down the ramp saying, "Don't sue me if something happens."

"The jerk! He had no right to hit you!" I reach out and pet Tess's lathered neck. She's trembling. "It's all right, Tess. Everything's all right." Next to her a huge cow moos, its long pink tongue outstretched. I run my palm along my mare's bumpy, wet, infected skin. "I dreamed about you last night," I say. "You carried me into the crashing ocean. You were so brave."

As I talk and pet her, she gradually calms down. She nuzzles my stomach. She shoves her nose beneath my arm.

"Let's get you out of here." I offer her a carrot. As she reaches to take it, I unsnap her lead rope. Turning to guide her out, I hear her hooves scrambling on the floor behind me.

Dad shouts, "Look out!"

Tess's shoulder catches me. She knocks me sideways off the ramp. But I keep to my feet. I hold on to her as she drags me through the men, past Dad's car and halfway up the hill to Granddad's house. I get her stopped all right.

When I lead Tess past Dad, she's so nervous she tosses her head, throwing foam on him. He brushes it off. He looks mad. I don't know what to say.

He takes a deep breath. I can almost hear him count to ten, trying to curb his anger. *He doesn't like my horse.* Oh why'd he have to come home now? Why not later, when she'd be bedded down and quiet in her big box stall?

That night, a thunderstorm erupts outside Granddad's house. Rain that I'd been praying for slashes against the windows. The wind flattens trees. Boswell hides beneath the sofa while Dad paces back and forth across the living room rug, his polished shoes black against the rug's pink roses.

"She almost killed you. That horse almost killed you. If I hadn't shouted, she would have trampled you."

"No, Dad! Horses don't trample people. Not if they can help it. She was frightened! In her stall, she was so scared she retreated to a corner. Not even Toby could get her to come out."

"When I saw you pull the driver aside to unload her yourself, do you know what I did?" Dad stops pacing to face me. "I took out the travel money I had in my wallet and counted it. Three hundred dollars. I was ready to give it to the driver just to haul the horse back where she came from!"

"But you didn't," Granddad says. He's sitting in his brown leather chair. On the table beside it are two drinks, his and Dad's. I watched Granddad make those drinks with soda water and a slice of lime. Dad didn't ask for a jigger of scotch in his—thank goodness.

"I must be crazy." Dad runs a hand through his thinning hair. "I'm returning to California next week—my project's been accepted. I'll be gone four months and—"

"You're going away again?" I say. "But you're always going away! I want us to be a normal family with you and me and Granddad—"

"That's not the point," Dad says. "The point is, I'll be leaving you with a horse you can't control."

"Tess is a good-hearted horse," Granddad says calmly. "She just needs time to settle down. I recommend we give her and Willo a week together. By then, we should know if they're suited."

"But Granddad! A week may not be long enough!"

"How much time do you want?" Dad says. "Three months? A year? Seven years? I know you, Willojean. Once you sink your teeth into something, you don't let go.

"We'll give it the week." Dad reaches out. He touches my cheek. I'm beginning to panic. I have only one week to settle Tess, and at the end of that week, my dad's leaving me. Again.

CHAPTER
6

The next morning, Dad's laptop computer, printer and diagrams of his project, the A-22 Stealth Intruder, cover the dining room table, except for the small space where I am eating cereal. The smell of coffee and frying bacon comes from the kitchen, where Granddad's "rustling up grub for the troops."

"What do you think of all this?" Dad sweeps his arm above the diagrams as if he's a ringmaster introducing the greatest act on earth.

"They remind me of a prehistoric skeleton. A pterodactyl. Something like that." I take the cereal bowl in both hands and drink the remaining milk.

"That's certainly an interesting comparison. Ptero-dactyls flew poorly, did you know? The Stealth Intruder won't. It could be the greatest spy plane in the U.S. Navy! But my team needs to perfect the de-sign. And come up with something—some kind of material—that's strong, yet soft enough to be worked and shaped. It's a tall order when you only have until November second."

"You can do it, Dad." To me, having just a week with Tess, November 2 seems light-years away. I push myself back from the table. "Gotta run."

"Where are you off to?"

"The barn. I have a horse to feed."

In the kitchen, I snitch a piece of bacon from a plate Granddad's set out on the little table where we eat when there's just us two.

"How about an egg?" he says.

"Not today, Granddad." I'm out the door and he's calling after me, "Don't you want a muffin?"

"No thanks." Outside the air feels cool and clean. Unlike hot and stuffy yesterday. My feet fly, carrying me downhill to the barn. Over to my right, a thousand wet Christmas trees glitter in sunlight.

"A horse, a horse, my kingdom for a horse," I chant as I run. According to the Shakespeare play, it was the last thing King Richard III said before dying on the battlefield. Mom, who'd been a librarian and knew about these things, told me, "King Richard would have won the battle of Bosworth Field and lived—if he'd only had a horse."

In the barn, Toby sticks out his head and nickers. *Oh boy. Here's Willo. Bring on the oats and sweetfeed.* My horse—the horse I'd give a kingdom for—flattens her ears at the sight of me. No more retreating into dark corners for Tess.

I feed Toby first so Tess can watch how we go through our morning ritual. Toby nuzzles my hair, my shirt, my jeans—searching for the pail of food I've hidden behind my back. "Love me, Toby?"

He shoves his head against my belly and snorts.

"You silly pony." I kiss the swirl of white caught in the middle of his brown forehead and then pour grain into his feed bin.

When I approach Tess with breakfast, she bares her teeth.

"What's wrong with you?" I jiggle the pail of grain. "Aren't you hungry?" She flicks her ears forward, but then, as I draw closer, flattens them.

"I'm not afraid of you." Using the bucket as a shield, I walk up to Tess. Blowing loudly out of her nostrils, she backs off. She watches me dump grain into her feed bin. I step back and she attacks her breakfast.

"Take it easy." I say the words to calm myself as well as Tess. I didn't know she'd be so scary.

Once she's eaten, she becomes a little friendlier. She lets me approach. She allows me to snap a lead shank to her halter so that I can lead her out of her stall. As I do, I turn around to close the door. By accident, I drop the end of the leather shank. She steps forward onto it and the shank brings her up short.

Throwing her head, she struggles against a shank she holds down with her own front hoof! She panics and tries to rear. Her hind legs scramble for purchase on the barn aisle's concrete floor. Her hind hooves slip. The shank doesn't give, but the halter does. She goes down on her rump, breaking her brand-new halter in two places.

"Please, Tess. Settle down," I tell her half an hour later. It's taken me that long to calm us both and repair her halter with baling twine. Now I've got her hitched to crossties while I try to brush off the manure stains covering her ribs and belly. I don't know what to do with her. Every time I brush, she raises her hind hoof, threatening to swipe my hand.

"The stains will cause sores. The sores will fester. You'll get another fever." I try to brush her belly again. She raises her hoof.

I throw the brush aside. What to do? I decide to comb out her knotted forelock. Maybe she'll like that. She rubs her head against the metal comb. The teeth of the comb come up against bumps. I part her forelock and discover the bumps are ticks. Some are fat and gray—ballooned with blood.

Tess rubs her head against my chest and I back off. I don't want to touch ticks. I hate ticks! Tess stretches out her neck. For the first time since she arrived at Mas-Que, Tess reaches out and nuzzles me.

"You want me to pull out the ticks."

She rests her soft gray muzzle against my stomach. I take a deep breath. "Okay."

Fifteen minutes later, Diana arrives in her red sports car. On Thursday, I'd called to tell her about Tess, and now, she's here. I can hardly wait for her to cross the barnyard. Oh, I hope she likes Tess!

"I picked out thirty-seven ticks from her forelock and mane," I tell Diana.

"Good for you. She must feel so much better now." Diana pets Tess's forehead while staring at her matted coat. I feel ashamed. I should have cleaned it off. "You've had a rough life, haven't you," Diana tells Tess. "And what have you done to your halter?"

"She broke it." I explain how. "She's a little skittish. But she'll calm down."

"Of course she will." Diana examines Tess closely, running her hand along my mare's skinny neck. She checks Tess's forelegs. She draws in her breath at the saddle sores and barbed-wire cuts. She touches a manure stain on Tess's flank. Tess raises a warning hoof. I wish she wouldn't do that.

"She won't let me brush her there," I say.

Diana looks over at me. "She has no fat, Willo. When you brush, it feels as if you're brushing her bones."

"Oh. I hadn't thought of that."

She cups Tess's muzzle in her hands. "What can we do for you? How can we help you?"

I like how Diana talks to Tess. I like how she says "we."

Tess breathes softly in and out against Diana's hands. She has beautiful long-fingered hands. I've seen these hands calm a frightened Sultan. I've felt them circling my back—calming me at my mom's funeral. Diana says, "Your mare tells me, if we're very careful, we could bathe her."

"You have time? You'll help?" She likes Tess! I can tell she likes her.

Without hesitating, she says, "I'd love to."

In the barnyard, we wash my mare with sun-warmed water from the large stone drinking trough. The water turns brown as it washes away Tess's manure stains. With lowered head and closed eyes, she allows us to gently sponge her neck, her spine, her ribs and her hips, which jut out as sharp as elbows. She's so gentle now. Like she was the first time I saw her.

"The vet says I'm not to ride her for a few days," I say, putting antibiotic cream on her saddle sores while Diana washes out her tail.

"Good. That will give you time to get to know each other." Over Tess's razorlike backbone, Diana surveys the barnyard with its corncrib, rolls of old fencing, storage shed, pigpen and farm machinery. "Where do you plan to ride her?"

"Around the farm, I guess."

"She's an ex-racehorse. She's skittish. She could be tricky to control." Diana says this, not as if she's telling me something I don't already know, but like she's thinking to herself out loud. She looks over at me. "There's a pasture I saw on my way in here. After that large hilly field with the silo."

"That's the old sheep's pasture."

"If she were my horse, I'd school her there. It's good and flat. No steep slopes to give her an excuse to run away." Diana pats Tess's rump. "Okay, my beauty. You're done."

Uphill, Dad's car backs out of the drive in front of Granddad's house. I call, "Hey Dad! Come see my horse!"

The car turns and Dad calls out the window, "No time, Willo. Maybe later." He heads down the driveway.

"He just came home from California," I explain. I can't seem to keep the disappointment out of my voice. I wanted him to see Tess. "Next Thursday, he has to go back. He'll be gone until November."

"He must have a lot to do." Diana steps back to look at the horse my dad does not have time to see. The sun glistens off her wet bay coat. It clings so tightly to her bones. In her broken halter, she holds her head up the way I love—high and proud. *Go on. Look! Look at me.*

"Isn't she beautiful?" I say.

"She certainly is," Diana says, and she hugs me.

CHAPTER
7

The sky's bright blue. The air smells of cut grass. Tess jerks against the lead shank. I laugh as my prancing mare pulls me up the road to Granddad's house. I've had Tess two days and she's all excited. Me, too. This is our first foray together into the world outside the barnyard! Tess grabs at apple tree branches. She shies at Boswell—darting across the road in front of her. She snorts. *What do we have here?*

"It's a cat, Tess." She carries on as if this cat's the most astounding creature she's ever seen. Boswell leaps on top of Granddad's battered gray car and fixes Tess with his pale green eyes. Tess pulls me across the drive-

45

way and plunges her head into a thick patch of grass growing in the side yard.

I sit down on a huge gray boulder, which according to Granddad, was part of a meteorite that had streaked through outer space. Tess is too intent on eating to be startled by it. I imagine each mouthful of grass she takes turning into a soft cushion of fat that fills in her hollows. I like to watch Tess eat.

I wish Dad could see her now. She's settling in. She's acting like a normal horse. Why'd he have to go to Baltimore today? Company headquarters shouldn't be open on a Sunday. All Dad left behind were orders for me: make my bed; pick my clothes up off the floor; clean off my boots and, next time, take them off before I come inside the house. They stink.

However, he did leave me two surprises to sweeten those orders—a box of chocolates to fatten me up and a book of poetry from the British Isles. The book is fat, unlike Tess or me, and it has Dad's and my favorite poem in it—"The Darkling Thrush," by Thomas Hardy.

"Ahoy there!" Granddad calls from an upstairs window.

I salute him. Tess raises her head and nickers. But she's not looking at Granddad. Her head's turned in the direction of the highway. I hear hoofbeats coming down our road. Who is it? Dove's still at the beach. Toby's in the barn.

Tess nickers again. It's Cloudy! Colin Wolf is riding the dappled gray gelding down our road. Am I in heaven or what? Diana came yesterday. Colin's here today.

He's never ridden to Mas-Que. It's not a long ride—only about three miles. But it's tricky, because for part of the way, you have to ride along Ferry Highway, which has narrow shoulders and too many trucks. Did Colin brave those trucks just to see Tess and me?

He rounds the pump house and halts Cloudy at the edge of Granddad's yard.

"Hi Colin," I say, and he says, "Hi. Boy is she skinny."

"She's getting fatter by the minute. You should see her eat." Tess pulls me to Cloudy. She sweetly nuzzles his neck, then she bites him.

"Tess!" I yank her back.

"Want to go riding?" Colin says, brushing off the bite. His red hair curls out from beneath a faded brown hard hat that brings out his hazel eyes. He wears a gray-blue shirt. The colors make me think of autumn—its wind-tossed sky, the leaves. I want to ride with Colin more than anything.

"I can't. Not until Wednesday." Tess pulls at the lead

shank. I loosen my hold slightly. She sniffs noses with Cloudy.

"Mom said you two seem to fit together," Colin says.

Maybe she can talk to Dad about it.

The screen door bangs open and Granddad comes outside. He puts his hand on my shoulder and says, "Colin Wolf. I was just talking to your stepfather yesterday. He says he wants to buy my farm."

Granddad speaks in a joking sort of way, but Colin takes it seriously. His face turns red. "He wants to buy everyone's farm."

"Well, he is in real estate," I say. Jack must do pretty well buying and selling farms and houses. He wears gold chains around his neck. He's always off somewhere playing golf. Most people seem to like him. He throws fancy parties. He has two huge tents and serves champagne at his Fourth of July party. "But Granddad will never sell Mas-Que," I add.

Granddad ruffles my hair. Tess drops her head and resumes eating grass. Cloudy drops his head and joins her—two gray muzzles, only inches apart.

"How'd you get the horse here?" Granddad asks Colin.

"I rode him through Mr. Condon's place, then I cut through the woods at the head of the creek."

"You did?" I thought he'd taken the highway. "But it's so swampy back there."

"I found a path. Only a small part goes through swamp. The rest runs along a ridge and down into a hollow."

"My cows made that path," Granddad says. "If you stick to it, you're fine. But for God's sake, don't venture off it. There's quicksand back there.

"We call that place the Confederates' Swamp," he continues. "During the Civil War, Confederate soldiers camped back there. Every so often, the swamp spits up artifacts—canteens, mule shoes. There's an old spring—a broken-down brick well—where the soldiers got their water."

"Granddad! You never told me about this!"

"Didn't I?" He scratches his head. "Guess I didn't want you fooling around back there. Still don't. Especially not with Tess."

But I want to fool around back there. I want to ride through the swamp with Colin. The sun glints off the ends of his hair. It makes it look as if it burns with fire.

"Willo." Granddad gives me the admiral's stare. He knows what I'm thinking. "The Confederates' Swamp is no place for a skittish horse. I don't want you and Tess back there."

"Yessir." I wish he wouldn't give me orders like this

in front of Colin. When people do this sort of thing to me, it makes me want to disobey them. Even Granddad.

A warm wind breaks against my face as I track the hoofprints Colin's horse made in Mas-Que's graveled driveway. Tess naps in the barn, but I'm too restless to sleep. I plan to track the hoofprints all the way through the Confederates' Swamp to Colin's house. I want to go where he's been, see what he's seen.

I break into a jog, my sneakers kicking up stones. To my right, a flock of wild ducks startles me—quacking loudly as they lift off Crazy's Pond. It's a patch of stagnant water, dead trees and mud the farm road skirts to get to the highway.

The pond's named for the Crazy Cow. She was a throwback, brindle-colored with horns like a bull. She protected Granddad's herd from wild dogs and cattle poachers. But for some reason no one knows, one day she barreled headlong into the pond and never came back out.

"Hello, you old Crazy Cow!" I call. Nothing echoes back. Shivering, I break into a run—away from the pond and uphill. To my left, the wind makes waves of the tall timothy Granddad will cut to make hay for Tess. To my right towers the broken-down silo that marks the edge of the big front field where Granddad's cattle used to graze.

Cloudy's suddenly wide-spaced hoofprints make it look as if he broke into a canter here. I love a rocking canter. I turn right into the field and imagine myself riding Cloudy. I sit in the saddle behind Colin and my arms are wrapped around his waist. My cheek is pressed against his back. I can hear his heartbeat.

Cloudy carries us past the spooky silo. It's full of water the color of dark beer. It stinks like beer. Last summer I found a dead raccoon floating inside it. I haven't been near the silo since.

I can feel my heart beating against Colin's. *Da-dump. Da-dump.* Two heartbeats turning into one. All in time to Cloudy's cantering. He carries us through a field gone wild with knee-high grass and scrub trees. I hear highway traffic—loud trucks barreling down the highway on my left.

Snorting, Cloudy stops at a break in the barbed-wire fence. The woods on the other side look so dark. They smell of swamp—mud and rotting weeds. A path edged with briars plunges downhill. I see crumbled brick along it. The old well? It looks like a well. Deerflies! A thousand bloodsucking deerflies swarm out of the swampy woods at me. One buzzes at my ear—*Let me in.*

Suddenly, Cloudy's gone. Colin's gone. The dream has died and there's just me, the path ahead leading past a break in the fence to the Confederates' Swamp and deerflies. A huge fly bites my neck. Another lands on my cheek! I go crazy. I scream. I shouldn't have come here! Waving my hands to ward off flies, I turn away from the swamp. With deerflies chasing after me, I head for Granddad's house at a flat-out run.

CHAPTER
8

Last November, Dad wrapped Mom in a thick gray blanket to keep her warm and he took us sailing down the creek and into Wyndham River. A northwest wind was blowing. It filled the *Bonnie Prince Charlie*'s sails and Dad's boat flew, heeling over until water just about buried its rail.

I braced my feet against the sloping deck and shouted, "Slow down, Dad! You're going to tip us over!"

"Relax!" he called through the wind. "I've got this baby in control and where I want her. On the edge and flying." The wind blew back his hair. Brackish water spotted his glasses. He was happy, sailing fast with Mom and me.

I was scared. Mom opened her blanket to let me snuggle in beside her. She smelled of Blue-Grass Cologne, and inside her Blue-Grass-smelling blanket tent, we huddled close. The *Bonnie Prince* practically stood up on its side rail as it cut through the white-capped waves.

"He'll tip us over," I said to Mom.

"No he won't. See how he handles the lines and sails? He knows how to use the wind and our body weight to keep everything in balance." A spray of water hit our faces and Mom laughed. "He loves to ride the wind. Just like you love riding horses."

Mom looked at Dad as she said this. He was securing a line. He grabbed the tiller and sat back. She said, "Roger, promise me something?"

His eyes rested on hers. "Anything."

"A horse for Willo?" She'd asked him this before. Each time, Dad had put her off. He didn't think I rode well enough. But how could he tell? He'd never seen me ride.

"She can have a horse." He said it now so easily I didn't believe him.

"Really, Dad? Promise?" If Dad promised, I knew this was real and for eternity.

"I promise." His eyes were still on Mom's.

Yes! I thought. Yes! Beneath the blanket, Mom hugged me. She was often in pain during the afternoon, but today, she didn't let on. She wanted everyone to be happy—this last time she went sailing.

Dad pushed the tiller away from him to adjust our course. With Mom between us, he headed the *Bonnie Prince* on a long tack down the river, which reflected all the pretty green, red, brown, yellow and orange leaves of fall. It was hard to tell where water ended and land began.

"Look!" Mom said. "Mares' tails!" She pointed to white wisps of clouds high in the blue sky above the *Bonnie Prince*'s taut sails.

Dad, squinting at those mares' tails, sang Mom's and my favorite song—

> *Way up yonder above the sky,*
> *A bay mare pranced in a blue jay's eye.*
> *Buckeye Jim, you can't go,*
> *Go weave and spin, you can't go,*
> *Buckeye Jim.*

I was so happy. Dad was singing. He'd promised me a horse. He sang another verse of Buckeye Jim and Mom and I joined in. It was a perfect day with the greatest parents in the world. Why did it have to end?

My mare's tail now swishes me. I'm tightening Tess's girth and she doesn't like it. I'm about to ride her for the second time in my life and the first time with Dove. Tess stomps her hind foot. I give the girth a final pull, then buckle it. "There. All done."

Dove knees Toby's puffed-out belly. "He's such a stinker." He exhales and she tightens his girth before he can inhale and grow fat again. For the third time. "Whew," she says. "I'm done in. Where do you want to ride?"

"The sheep's pasture?" I promised Granddad that until Tess and I got used to each other, I'd ride her there. It's probably not a bad idea. She gets excited by little things like scraps of paper and I'm not sure I know how to calm her. "But let's stop at the house first," I tell Dove. "I want Dad to see Tess."

Dad's been so busy working in Baltimore on the Stealth Intruder, he hasn't seen the horse he promised I could have since she arrived. Now it's July 4 and Dad's leaving tomorrow. He's got to see my horse! I've worked hard with Tess and it shows. Her coat's taken on a shine. Fuzzy hair's starting to cover her scars.

Outside the barn, the morning sun shines through a hazy sky. The heat, which had backed off for a few days, has returned in full battle force. Already, I can tell it's going to be the kind of day when your skin grows so clammy it can't breathe. The manure pile in front of the barn stinks.

Dove holds Tess still for me so that I can mount.

Once I'm on board, my ex-racehorse trots off to Granddad's house. Through stiff new leather reins, I feel her mouthing the snaffle bit I bought her. It's a gentle bit. It won't make her mouth bleed. Tess throws her head. The edges of the reins cut into my little fingers.

"Well, look who's come to see me!" Josefa calls from the kitchen window. Dove's grandma came today to help us out—doing Dad's laundry before he leaves for California and baking cookies for Gram. She's my dad's mom. Gram lives on the Eastern Shore and Dad and I will be celebrating the Fourth of July with her.

"So this is Tess." Josefa hands Dove and me chocolate chip cookies hot from the oven. Tess paws the ground, eager to be off. I notice how Josefa backs away, putting a safe distance between herself and my restless horse.

"Tess isn't mean. You can pet her," I say.

"Grandma's a little afraid of horses," Dove explains.

I'm surprised. Josefa works part-time as a practical nurse. I've seen her give shots. Adjust IVs. Bathe Mom. She cradled Mom's head to feed her, and near the end, prayed for her while she was dying. I didn't think Josefa was afraid of anything.

"Where's Dad?" I ask Josefa. I'd told him I was coming.

"He's with your grandpa, walking the fields." A

smile covers Josefa's broad face. "They want to plant the rest of the farm in Christmas trees. This is what your mama wanted. This will make her happy."

"But I told Dad to wait here!"

"His head's so full of all he has to do, your papa forgot."

"Don't worry," Dove says. "The farm's not that big. We'll find him, Willo."

Dad was the one who was concerned about Tess. Now I'll have to ride my anxious mare all over Mas-Que to find him. What if Tess panics? What if she runs away? We head out down the driveway. The only sounds are clopping hooves, Tess's swishing tail and the jingle of seven silver bracelets Dove bought at the beach. I wish she hadn't worn them today. The sound makes Tess uneasy. She sidles across the crown of the driveway and over to its shoulder.

Maybe Dad and Granddad will be in the sheep's pasture—inspecting the flats of seedling pines we heeled in beside the old sheep's shed. I'll ride Tess around the field for Dad. He'll smile as I put her through her paces.

He and Granddad aren't there! Dove and I trot our horses out of the pasture and down the road past Crazy's Pond. Dove's bracelets jangle. Tess tosses her head. She throws spit, the color of the hazy sky, on me. "Easy, girl."

We reach the end of Mas-Que's driveway without seeing anyone. Blackberry bushes growing along the edge of the highway hang heavy with berries and with heat. Bees buzz. The sun glares off the mailbox. A truck roars past. Tess pivots. Why couldn't Dad have waited at the house to see her?

"Let's head back," I tell Dove. I need to get Tess into the sheep's pasture. She dances excitedly from one foreleg to another. A second truck roars past.

"Willo!" Dove says. "There they are! Next to the silo!"

"They must have been in the woods." I'm so happy we found Dad and Granddad. "Let's trot over to them." Long-legged Tess moves right out. Her neck stretches out. I feel a gentle weight on the bit—no hard pulling. I post well to her proud trot. *Look at us, Dad!*

Toby breaks into a canter to keep up with Tess. For several strides he's neck to neck with her. Then he passes Tess. He shouldn't pass Tess. She's an ex-racehorse! She leans on her bit—*Let me at him.* Her withers seem to stand on end.

"No, Tess." Shortening the reins, I pull back. Instead of slowing, Tess extends her trot. I find myself standing in the stirrups, sawing on the reins. *Slow down! Oh, I don't want Dad to see this.*

Ahead of me, Dove rises in her stirrups, too. She saws on Toby's reins, but now that we're headed in the direction of Toby's favorite place—the barn, with its barrels of oats and sweetfeed—Toby doesn't listen. He flattens out into a gallop.

I try to turn Tess toward the wild field and Dad, but she ducks her head, throwing me off balance. I fall back into the saddle and Tess breaks into a canter. Before I can gather up the reins again, Tess grabs the bit between her teeth. Dad and Granddad stand there watching and Tess explodes, tearing after Toby.

She passes him so fast I can't feel her legs moving beneath me. She rounds a bend in the road and hurtles past Crazy's Pond at a million miles an hour. The wind whips against my face. "Stop, Tess," I moan.

Where the road forks—the left branch leading to Granddad's house, the right branch to the barn—Tess turns abruptly right. With me clinging to her neck, she gallops through the tunnel of apple trees and into the barnyard. This horse I'd give up a kingdom for stops at the manure pile. But I keep on going.

CHAPTER 9

It's hot in Dad's white Buick. Sweat drips down my neck. It makes the backs of my legs stick against the car seat. A bouquet of flowers Dad bought for Gram droops across my lap. For the past half hour, we've been caught in a traffic jam smack in the middle of the Chesapeake Bay Bridge and Dad's turned off the car's air-conditioning so that the engine won't over-heat.

"I don't believe it!" Dad pounds the heels of his hands against the steering wheel. "We leave at noon to avoid the morning rush and look what happens. She's going to be a mess. She'll be pacing the floor, certain we've died."

"I wish we had a car phone so we could call Gram," I say.

"Well, we don't." Dad fiddles with the radio, zapping one station, then the next. I want to be anywhere but in the car with him. He's like a firecracker, already lit and ready to explode. He often gets like this when we visit Gram. He did even when Mom was alive. Today, he's worse. Because of Tess running away with me. He hasn't said it, but I know he wants me to get rid of her; we don't belong together.

On either side of the car, steel cables rise toward the hazy sky. Hundreds of feet below, gray water glints in the sunlight. Looking at it makes the bottoms of my feet feel queasy. I look instead at the flowers in my lap—white and pink and droopy yellow. I should have stuck them in water. Why didn't I bring water?

"It's one hundred sweltering degrees out there," a radio announcer says. "If you have a heart condition, stay inside."

I have a heart condition all right. My dad wants me to sell my horse. He turns off the radio. He roots through the glove compartment, finds a cassette and slips it in the tape deck. Violins play and a man's voice sings:

Ae fond kiss, and then we sever;
Ae farewell, alas forever,
Deep in heart-wrung tears I'll pledge thee,
Warring sighs and groans I'll wage thee.

It's one of Dad's Scottish music tapes. He must have twenty of them. He loves Scotland. He and Mom went there on their honeymoon; he rode a horse with her across the Scottish moors. He never talks about that now, or about Mom. The song's sad and hearing it makes me even sadder. I can't give up the horse I love.

Now Dad's singing with the tape:

Had we never loved so kindly,
Had we never loved so blindly,
Never met—or never parted—
We had ne'er been brokenhearted.

"I love Tess. I won't be parted from her! I don't want to give Tess up!" I say.

Dad's hands grip the steering wheel so hard his knuckles turn white. "I leave for California tomorrow. I'll be gone until November second. The last thing I want to worry about is you with a horse you can't control."

"I'll learn to control her, Dad."

He stares out the car window.

Fair thee well, thou first and fairest,
Fair thee well, thou best and dearest
Thine be ilka joy and treasure,
Peace, enjoyment, love and pleasure.

"You should have seen Tess after I'd fallen off. She was so funny," I say, desperate to keep my horse. "I was sitting smack-dab in the middle of the manure pile. And do you know what Tess did?"

Dad doesn't answer, so I say, "She lowered her head and snorted—*How'd you end up there?*

"Tess followed me into the barn. I didn't have to lead her or anything. When I took off her saddle, she turned and nuzzled my hair." I am trying to be brave. Trying to make light of all that happened. It's not so bad. Horses run away with kids. Kids fall off. Granddad, who'd come to the barn to check on me, agreed.

"Tess isn't mean, Dad. Toby shouldn't have passed her . . . you don't pass an ex-racehorse—they're bred to win."

Why won't Dad speak? Say something. Anything. I hate his silent treatment. It feels like he's gone off somewhere far away and I can't reach him.

"Granddad told me, 'Just because you lose one skirmish, Willo, doesn't mean you lose the war.' All we need to do is beef up our battle tactics. He thinks maybe we should build a ring for me in the sheep's pasture. We have extra fencing. We can do it. I'll ride Tess there. If she runs away with me again, it'll be in circles."

Dad drums his fingers along the steering wheel. The words he doesn't say feel as if they're strangling me. I wish Granddad were here. He'd stick by me. But he's at his annual Independence Day poker game.

"Diana thinks Tess and I belong together," I say to Dad's hard silence. And then, more softly, "Mom would have thought so, too."

Dad, startled, glances at me. I don't believe I've mentioned Mom to him since she died. Mom's not someone we ever talk about. "What makes you say that?"

"She loved a horse with spirit."

Dad leans on his car horn then. Other horns join in. All the loud and sudden honking jars something loose. The car in front of us begins to move. Two long lines of cars begin to creep slowly across the bridge. On Dad's tape, bagpipes begin to wail. A hot wind blows through the car windows. It smells of gasoline and fish.

Gram's small cool dining room is smoky-smelling. She left bread in the oven for too long and it all burned up. Sunlight, glancing through closed lace curtains, casts shadow flowers on the table, neatly set with folded napkins, forks, knives, spoons and paper plates holding ham, potato salad and red Jell-O with sliced cucumbers in it.

"Sit down. Sit down," Gram says. "The food's already cold. Willo, you sit beside me. I want to hear all about you."

"I have a horse," I say.

"A horse. Isn't that nice." She smiles over at Dad. "You never had a horse, did you, Roger?"

"No, Mother." Dad doesn't smile back.

Gram dabs a napkin against her mouth, smearing her red lipstick. Her long white hair, which she'd tried to pull back into a bun, has come undone. If Dad weren't at the table with us, I'd fix it for her.

"But your father let you have a dog," Gram says. She stares at the portrait of Dad's father—my Grandfather Arthur—that hangs on the wall behind Dad. Grandfather Arthur has a fat face and small mean eyes. "Skipper," Gram goes on. "The dog's name was Skipper. He was a sweet dog. What's your horse's name, Willo?"

"Tess."

Gram leans close to me. I can smell her breath. Peppermint. When Gram eats peppermint, she's usually covering up the scent of whiskey. I hope she doesn't have any more whiskey in the house. I feel my stomach twist. "Is Tess a pretty horse?" she says.

"She has a beautiful face, with a white star and stripe. She has large dark eyes—"

"Skipper was a pretty dog," Gram says. "Roger found him. Someone must have tossed him out of a car. He had a broken leg. We took him to the vet and he put Skipper's little leg in a cast. Every time he climbed down the steps, the cast would go thump, thump, thump.

"He slept in bed with Roger. Arthur had a fit." Gram spears a jellied cucumber with her fork. When she tries to eat it, red Jell-O drips down her chin. I hand her my napkin, because hers is smeared with lipstick.

She smiles, wipes her chin and puts the napkin in her lap. "That Skipper. What a dog. Except Arthur scared him. Skipper only peed on the floor once."

"Mother, don't go into this." Dad gets up from the table.

"Only once." Tears glisten in Gram's eyes. "You could have trained Skipper not to pee like that. All you needed was a little time," she says, and Dad walks out of the room.

"Don't cry, Gram." I pet her hand. Her white skin feels like paper, thin and fragile.

"Arthur says there's no room in this world for imperfection." Gram speaks as if my grandfather is still alive. He died before I was born. "Roger only had Skipper a week and Arthur made him give the puppy to the dog pound. Roger was just a little boy. He cried and cried.

"Ah well. Chin in and belly up." Gram throws her shoulders back and nods to me. "All right, my girlie. Eat up. I think you'll like your Jell-O. I added a little sherry to it. It'll make your hair curl."

Dad returns as I am taking my first bite. He carries two drinks—each with a twist of lemon and a cherry in it. The drinks are made with whiskey. I can tell. I know the signs. Dad hasn't had a drink of whiskey since mid-January. He shouldn't be having one now. Gram's cucumber Jell-O sticks in my throat.

"One drink for you." Dad places a glass next to Gram's plate. "And one drink for me." He places the other glass next to his.

"Old-fashioned cocktails!" Gram chortles. "Our favorites."

Fireworks explode through the sky outside our speeding car. Trails of colored smoke spider the night. Dad turns the steering wheel to negotiate a curve in the long dark road. The car tires squeal. I grip the door handle and bite down on a scream that's building up inside me. I mustn't scream when Dad is drunk. Screams make him drive faster.

Why'd he have to drink tonight? One drink always

leads to another. And another. He can't stop. He knows that. After Mom's funeral, he told me, "It's just you and me now, Willo. I'll be a good father. I'll take care of you. No more drinks for me." I believed him.

But he didn't promise. I should have made him promise.

Wind tears at my hair. The road straightens out and Dad rests his elbow on the open car window. He's steering with one hand. The speedometer says he's driving eighty miles an hour.

"Slow down, Dad!"

He floors the accelerator.

"Dad!" I scream.

Eighty-five. Ninety. Ninety-five. Outside, another firework sets off the night. Another. And another. White rockets of light explode into pink, green, blue, red and yellow stars. Stars are falling—

Slow down, Dad. Please.

"It's no use, Willo." Dad says each word too distinctly. The car stinks of his whiskey breath. Rotteny whiskey.

"What's no use?" I whisper to the night, because to talk out loud to Dad might make him drive even faster.

"Controlling life."

Controlling life? What's he talking about? Why can't he drive slower? *Please drive slower.* Outside the car, fireworks are exploding.

"You'll never control Tess," he says.

"Yes I will," I say softly. "I can train Tess, Dad. Just like you could have trained Skipper. If Grandfather hadn't been so mean. If only Grandfather had given you the time."

"Time?" Dad says. The car seat shifts. Dad's turned. The car's approaching a country bridge at a million miles an hour and Dad's not looking at the bridge, but at me. "How much time, Willo?"

I don't know what to say.

"How much, Willo?" His foot flattens the accelerator to the floor. We're going so fast the car's shaking.

I blurt out a date that's been at the back of my mind ever since he mentioned it, a date I know means a lot to him. "Give me until you come home . . . November second."

"November second." Dad slows the car from ninety-five miles per hour to eighty. In the fireworked night, his face takes on an eerie glow.

"Yessir."

"My deadline for the Stealth Intruder. You want that deadline, too. For Tess." He shakes his head, a smile playing at the corners of his mouth. "It will give us something in common, won't it. Something to talk about." The car slows to seventy miles an hour.

"Shake on it." Dad holds out his hand. I hesitate.

Ahead of us, a concrete bridge soars upward into an explosive night.

Dad says, "Seal it, Willo."

I reach out my hand. His hand, engulfing mine, is cool and hard and dry. The car slows to fifty-five miles an hour. We're on the bridge now. A smoky wind blows through our windows. It smells like Gram's burned bread.

CHAPTER
10

When I wake up the next morning, I feel like a rubber band that's been stretched out as far as it can go and then released. There's nothing steady about me except my heart. It aches.

In my shade-darkened room, a rotating fan blows gusts of hot air across my bed. It's going to be another sweaty day. The luminous numbers on my alarm clock say 11:15 A.M. Dad's flight left at ten. He'll be gone four months and he didn't even wake me up to say good-bye.

I hate it when people don't say good-bye. "Good-bye" means *God be with you.* What if something bad like cancer happens and you don't see each other again? Will God be with you? No. You'll roast in hell!

On rubbery legs, I make my way downstairs. Every morning since the New Year, I've pretended to be a jumper. I've tried to clear the landing outside Grand-dad's office, which we'd used as a bedroom for my mom. Today, I'm so tired I step right on the landing. The floorboards creak the way they did each time we rolled Mom's oxygen machine across them. How can we go on without her?

In the kitchen, Granddad glances up from his newspaper. "Well, look what the cat dragged in."

"I'm hot." I get out milk and let the open refriger-ator cool me off before I close the door.

Granddad goes back to reading and I eat cereal. The rice puffs bob in milk like little storm-tossed ships at sea. "I drove our C.O. to the airport," Granddad says. "Seems we're to build you a riding ring."

"Dad agreed to that?" I say to my cereal.

"He did. He also left orders. You're not to ride Tess anywhere but in the ring. He wants you to lead her to it and back."

"Yessir." I stir the cereal. The rice puffs sink, but they bob up again.

"Willo. Look at me."

Granddad's eyes are soft with understanding. I love him so. "It's no use wallowing in yesterday's defeat,

Willo," he says. "We need to marshal the troops. I'll call my good friends Al and Harry. Line them up to build you the ring. You call Diana. Get some of those grand-slam riding lessons set up."

"Yessir." I'm afraid to call Diana. She's my teacher. She knows how well I ride. What if, after hearing what's happened, she says Tess is too much of a horse for me?

Hands trembling, I dial a number that I know by heart—263-6181. Diana picks up the phone on the first ring. As soon as I say, "Hi," she says, "What's wrong?"

"Tess ran away with me and I fell off." My voice chokes. I feel like I'm about to cry. I don't say, "And Dad's left. He'll be gone for the next four months and he didn't even say good-bye."

"Did you get hurt?" Diana sounds so caring—like a mom.

"No. Tess dumped me in the manure pile."

Diana chuckles. "The first time a horse threw me, I landed in a mud puddle."

"You fell off?"

"We can't call ourselves riders until we do. The trick is getting back on. You need to get back on Tess and we need to set up some lessons for you. I have a slot free. I could be at your farm at eight A.M. next Friday. We could work in that flat area—"

"The sheep's pasture! Granddad's building a ring for me there." Maybe things will work out after all. Diana's willing to help. With Diana, I feel I can accomplish anything.

Dove's already at the barn by the time I arrive. She has Toby hitched to crossties. While I tell Dove about Tess's deadline and my riding ring, she braids silver, red and blue ribbons through Toby's thick dark mane. She's turning him into "a Fourth of July Independence Day pony—one day late."

"I'll school Toby in the ring with you," she says as she works glittery gel through his forelock. She stops and looks at me. "I'm sorry for what happened yesterday."

"I know."

"I won't ever let Toby pass Tess again." Dove pulls his gelled forelock up through her hands. His hair stands straight up. "What do you think?"

"It makes him look surprised."

Dove kisses Toby's nose. "You funny whiskers." To me she says, "You're lucky you missed the Wolfs' Fourth of July party."

Lucky? I was stuck in a speeding car. "What do you mean?"

"Colin and Jack got into a fight. It was so stupid. Jack asked Colin to get him a bottle opener. Colin said,

'Get it yourself!' That made Jack so angry he grabbed Colin by the shirt collar and hauled him off to the house. Everyone was watching."

"Why didn't Colin just get the bottle opener?"

"Are you kidding? That would make life too easy for Jack. I sometimes wonder—if Colin had tried to be nicer to him, maybe Jack wouldn't have turned out to be so mean."

"I wonder why someone like Diana ever married him," I say.

"It was animal magnetism," Dove says. "It can really mess you up. It makes you think you're in love with someone, when you don't really know him."

Thinking of Colin, I blush.

"Hey," she says. "I fed Tess for you. I don't think she likes me."

"Sure she does. She just doesn't know how to show it." My throat aches as I say this.

"She tried to bite me."

"She wouldn't really bite you. She's all bluff. She's just trying to protect her stall. She's probably never had such a nice stall." Tess's box stall is really two stalls with the wall knocked out between them to make one. I always make certain it's covered with clean straw. The stall has a deep manger that can hold a half a bale of hay, all fluffed out and smelling sweet.

From her stall, Tess watches Dove, Toby and me. As

I approach my mare, she flattens her ears and bares her teeth. Why can't she act happy to see me? I've cared for her for almost a week. Doesn't she know that she can trust me?

The following Wednesday, a dark green pickup pulls into our driveway. *Let Al and Harry Do It!* is emblazoned on the driver's side. "Harry's a little gruff," Granddad warned me before heading out to cut the hayfield. "Al's the one to talk to. He's the more approachable one."

A big man with white hair climbs out of the cab. His one cheek bulges out. "You Willo?" he says. "You gonna show me where to build this ring?"

"Yessir." This must be Harry.

He hawks, then spits tobacco juice at the driveway. "Climb in." He nods toward the truck cab. Someone with a blue baseball cap pulled firmly down on his forehead sits inside. But it's not Al. It's Colin. I haven't seen Colin since he rode over to the farm. My cheeks turn red with the memory—imagining myself riding with him on Cloudy; my face was pressed against Colin's back.

"What are you doing here?" I say as I sit beside him on the hot truck seat.

"Pinch-hitting for Al. He broke his leg."

"Oh," I say, and then, "What happened to your

hand?" The knuckles on Colin's right hand are bruised and swollen.

"I rammed it through a door."

"That must have hurt."

Harry climbs in then and the truck seat sags. Colin moves closer to me. His leg rests against mine. I like the feel of his warm leg against mine. *Don't move. Please don't move.* His bruised hand rests on his knee. Why'd he ram his hand through a door? Did he get mad at someone? At Jack? Oh, I wish I could kiss Colin's hand and make everything all well. That's what my mom always did for me.

CHAPTER
11

"Jack always wants to know where Mom's at. Who she's with. What she's doing," Colin says as he jabs a posthole digger into the hard dry ground. Golden grass surrounds us on three sides. On the fourth stands the sheep's shed with its small paddock now holding seven flats of seedling Christmas trees. "He doesn't want her to visit anyone or do anything without clearing it with him first. The worst part is, she goes along with it. She does everything he says."

We are building my ring and Colin's talking to me about Diana, who'll give me lessons in it starting Friday. I wish he wouldn't tell me personal things about his mom. It's like he's unpeeling a beautiful orange in front of me, so that I can see the pulp inside. I don't like to see pulp. Diana's perfect as far as I'm concerned. I don't want to hear otherwise.

"Yesterday, Jack tacked up a sheet of paper on the kitchen door. On it, Mom's to log in where she's going, what time she leaves and when she's coming back. When I saw that, I got so mad I rammed my fist through the paper and the door as well.

"Mom was really upset. She said, 'When you lose your temper like that, you're no better than he is.' " Colin jabs his posthole digger deep.

"I get mad sometimes," I say.

"I don't believe it. You're too nice." He twists the digger, then snaps it shut to draw out the dirt.

"I'm not always nice. Once, I got so mad at my dad I took a jar of mayonnaise, raised it over my head and smashed it against the hall floor. It was awful. Mom was sick from chemotherapy. She was crying and there was all this glass and mayonnaise everywhere."

"Your mom was sick a long time," Colin says.

"First, it was her lungs. Then something went wrong with her throat and she couldn't eat or drink." I've never told Colin about this, although I've told Diana. When my mom was deep in pain and I didn't know what to do, Diana said, "Don't be afraid of her because she has cancer. Love her, Willo. Make every moment count." I'd often imagine Diana holding me and telling me that.

Colin's finished digging. He sticks a locust post in the hole. With a shovel, I start filling in the dirt around it. I smell dry dirt, warm grass and Colin. What would it be like to have Colin holding me?

"I'm riding Sultan now," he says.

"Really? I thought only your mom could ride him." I'd overheard Diana tell several students she couldn't give them lessons on Sultan. He was a one-person horse.

"I convinced her to let me try. Willo, it's like we were made for each other. I was only on him a few minutes and he came on the bit for me."

"What do you mean—on the bit?" I've never heard of this.

"When I take up the reins and move Sultan out, he leans on the bit, putting his weight in my hands. Allowing all his power to be controlled by these." Colin holds his hands up—one normal, the other all beat up. He curls his hands, as if they're holding reins. I imagine Sultan with arched neck and muscles gleaming, doing a sitting-trot beneath Colin. *On the bit.* I think this being on the bit is something I might want for Tess and me.

That night, I look up the expression in a book on horseback riding. According to the book, to get a horse on the bit you use your seat and legs to activate his hindquarters—sort of like revving up a car engine. The horse bends his head, leans on the bit, and the energy you've generated comes forward into your hands. If you are a sensitive and feeling person, the book says, you can help your horse collect this energy and use it—completing a flow of communication from him up to you and back again. It sounds magical to me. Once you get your horse on the bit, you can take just about anything that gets in your way. Like jumps.

"Last night, I took Sultan over a four-foot chicken coop," Colin says the next afternoon. The posts to my ring are in and the wire's been stretched and stapled between them. Now, while Harry's up at the house with Granddad, Colin and I hammer in a few remaining boards that go around the top.

"I believe Sultan would take on anything for me." Colin takes a nail out of his mouth and hammers it through the board I'm holding up for him. Our last board. I'm almost sad. We're so close I can smell Colin's breath. It smells sweet. Like grass.

"What does it feel like, jumping that high?"

"Incredible." Colin's eyes look into mine. He has

incredible eyes. Hazel with gold flecks. I could get lost in them. I blush and look away. Beyond him, seven flats of seedlings droop in the heat. I should water them.

"I want Tess to be a jumper. But first, I need to get her on the bit." I like how I can use this phrase so casually—as if I really understood it.

"Mom will teach you. Once you feel your horse is on the bit, you won't forget it, Willo. It's total communication. You're dancing."

Colin's sweaty arm brushes against mine and it feels like total communication. His sweat's mingling with mine. I won't wash my arm. Ever. With his hurt hand, he hammers in the last nail. "There. Your ring's done."

We both stand back to examine *my ring*. It's oblong—about sixty by a hundred feet. It's made of smooth wire—all these interconnected squares. It's topped by boards that I'll paint white. In this ring, I'll teach my horse about being on the bit. She'll come on the bit for me. She has to.

Colin puts his hammer away. He pushes his hat brim up and wipes his face with the edge of his T-shirt. Then he sits in the shade of a big old maple. It's near the seedlings that we plan to plant next spring in the wild field with the silo. And the little trees will watch me ride Tess through the field on my way to the Confederates' Swamp where I'll meet Colin. He'll be waiting there for me, in those dark woods, on Sultan.

I drag out the hose from the sheep's shed and start to water the seedlings. I can't see one without thinking of Mom. She loved the whole idea of growing Christmas trees. She said they bring such joy to dark December.

"You look hot," I call over to Colin. "Want a drink?"

"Sure." He gets to his feet. His eyes are on mine as he approaches.

"Trees need so much water," I say, now looking at the trees because I can't look at Colin. He makes me feel shy. "We set up a Christmas tree in Mom's bedroom, you know, last December? It was a live tree. Mom was always after us to water it."

Colin lowers his head to get a drink. Seeing him up close like this, the back of his neck so white against his thick red hair, makes my throat ache. "Something was wrong with Mom's throat," I say to keep on talking. "She could only whisper."

My voice trails off into a whisper as I watch how Colin's mouth cups the stream of water. How his throat moves. When he's finished, when he raises his head, I turn the hose on his hurt hand. I watch soothing water flow over Colin's bruised and swollen knuckles.

I look up to find Colin watching me. Something about the expression on his face reminds me of Diana. The half-smile? The sudden warmth in his eyes? He tilts his head. I tilt mine. I grin. "Hi."

"Hi," he says softly. His wet hand touches my cheek. While water pours onto the thirsty ground and all the little Christmas trees are watching, Colin runs his finger along my ski jump of a nose and over my mouth. He touches my chin. I don't move. I am as still as stone.

Slowly, gently—as if he's been doing this sort of thing all his life—Colin places his warm lips on mine. It's better than mixing sweat. The sweet taste makes me dizzy. I lean into him and I kiss back—*Don't stop. Don't ever stop.*

CHAPTER
12

At dusk, Maiden Creek is full of life. Bats darting. Fish jumping. Crabs swimming along the surface of the muddy-looking water. With lowered head, Tess blows out her nostrils at it. This is the first time I've led Tess down to the creek, and I can tell she likes it. With her foreleg, she splashes at her reflection.

"You silly horse." I take a handful of water and let it dribble over her back. Tess shivers and moves forward. She pulls me into the water until she's knee-deep and I'm up to my thighs. "Today, Colin kissed me, Tess. It was the grandest thing. It should have lasted longer. Why did Harry return so soon?"

I lean myself over Tess's back. Before I know what I'm doing, I've pulled myself up on her. Easy. One moment in the water, the next on Tess. I shouldn't have done this. I haven't ridden her since she ran away with me. Haven't yet ridden her in the ring. Granddad's there now, setting in the gate bolts he just bought.

Anyway, this isn't riding. It's . . . swimming. I'll call it swimming. I can feel Tess's bones. Her backbone. Those ribs. With my bare legs, I urge her deeper into the water. One step leads to another, and as the creek floor deepens, she half rears and sinks beneath me. I cling to her, afraid we'll both go under. She starts to swim! She does it so naturally, as if this is something she's been bred to do. I hold on to her mane and she calmly carries me past Dad's sailboat and toward a summer cottage where a dirt road leads to Colin's farm. Colin—the first boy ever to kiss me.

Tomorrow Diana, who's been teaching him to jump Sultan, will, for the first time, begin to teach Tess and me. By November 2, I'll have her on the bit. I'll be able to take her on trail rides. We'll be jumping!

We'll show Dad. Tess nears the broken-down dock, and before her hooves strike creek bottom, I lean the rope against her neck. She turns easily. She turns back. Like the sea, she surges beneath me, bringing me home. The water is warm—kissed by sunlight. As are the clouds. Orange, yellow and a dusky pink.

"They're discombobulated, those two," I overhear Granddad tell Diana the next morning. They've been watching me put Tess through her paces in my new ring. Tess only seems to have two—prance and run. When Tess prances, I bounce. When she runs, I almost bounce off. Diana has called out several times, "Sit deep in your saddle. Be firm with Tess. When you pull back, mean it."

When I sit deep and pull back, Tess lunges at the bit. She pulls me out of the saddle and onto her neck.

Now Diana asks me to try figure eights—up, around and down the ring. "It'll help to coordinate you," she says.

Tess prances and I bounce. We turn every figure eight into an uncoordinated zigzag.

When the lesson's over, Diana gives Tess and me things to work on—walking, trotting and cantering. We're to practice figure eights. If we don't get something right the first time, we're to try again the next day.

"Don't get discouraged," Diana says. "You two are on a mission to get to know each other." She looks at Granddad. "It will take patience. And time."

He nods to her. He understands.

I dismount to lead Tess to the barn, and for a moment, I slump against my mare. I hope Granddad and

Diana don't give up on Tess and me. I kiss the hollow over her left eye. She turns around and nuzzles my stomach.

Clouds hang heavy in the sky. There is no wind. The weather's hot and sultry. I've had two lessons with Diana now and Tess and I still don't know each other. I wish we had a lesson today, but Diana and Colin are in Massachusetts, where they're visiting Diana's relatives. I'm surprised Jack let them go. I hate that they went away. What if something happens and they don't come back?

But they will. And when they do, maybe I'll get a chance to be alone with Colin. It seems whenever I see him, either Dove or one of Colin's friends is there. Doesn't Colin want to be alone with me?

I kick at a green apple that's fallen off one of Granddad's trees. I bat the apple, first with my left foot, then with my right, batting it down the driveway toward the wild field with the silo where the horses have been grazing for the night.

Dad called home last night. "How's Tess?" he said.

"She's fine. How's the Stealth Intruder?"

"Coming fine. Everything is hunky-dory." Every word he said, he said too precisely, which meant to me that he'd been drinking whiskey again. I don't like to talk to him when he's been drinking.

I kick the apple hard. It bounces off a rock and lands, hunky-dory, in Crazy's Pond. A fleet of hungry deerflies swarms out of the marsh grass and bombards my head. Batting flies, I run uphill, and as I do, a bird sings out—"Eee-oo-lay."

Looking back, I see a little brown bird—a wood thrush—perched high in a dead tree smack in the middle of the pond. The bird raises his beak and he sings out a second time—"Eee-o-lay!" Below him, old dead leaves and a green apple float in pockets of dark water.

"I know a poem about you, thrush!" I call.

> I leant upon a coppice gate
> When Frost was spectre-gray,
> And Winter's dregs made desolate—

I only get through these three lines of "The Darkling Thrush," when the wood thrush sings out a third time and, in answer, the whole world seems to tremble. But it's not the world. Of course it's not the world. It's Tess. My bay mare charges through the wild field with the silo. She gallops toward the gate, her hooves pounding the grass she's fed on all night long.

I run to her, my feet kicking up gravel. A rail grazes my back as I climb through the gate to greet my mare. She slides to a stop about three yards away from me. "Hey Tess!"

She tosses her head. Eyes wild with excitement, she wheels and takes off in the other direction before I have the chance to say, "Wait! I've got carrots!" She charges past the silo to a thick patch of clover where Toby's grazing.

She prances around Toby as if he's the greatest thing alive. Why can't she feel like this about *me*? I open the gate and Toby raises his head. He nickers and trots toward me, his broad belly swaying. Tess, stock-still, watches him. As Toby's whiskery muzzle snuffles a carrot from my hand, Tess gives a sharp whinny.

"Ignore her," I say. "You've got me and I've got treats." Toby walks sedately beside me through the gate and back down the driveway. Moments later, Tess comes charging after him. Reaching Toby, she noses his back. She nips his neck. *How could you think of leaving me?*

In her stall, Tess goes through her usual ritual when I bring breakfast. I put her feed bucket on the floor and, as if I didn't notice her flattened ears, say, "Hungry, Tess?"

She thuds her hoof against the door.

"You've got to do better than that."

She throws her head. She paws the floor and bares her teeth.

"No! Enough of that!" I walk right up to her. I place

my hands on either side of Tess's mouth. She closes it. She grows so suddenly still. I feel her breathing in and out. I smell her breath—grass-sweet.

"Love me?" *Please love me.*

She rests her mouth against my shoulder. Will she bite me? I don't care. I rest my cheek against the side of her head. She shifts her weight. She flattens her upper lip against my collarbone. Afraid to move, I hold my breath. She leans her weight against me, and then she slowly runs the inside of her soft, moist upper lip down my shoulder and along my arm. I can't believe it. I am absolutely stunned.

She knocks her hoof against the door. *Enough of this lovey stuff.* But I don't move just yet. I can't.

CHAPTER 13

Kiss: v.t. 1. to caress with the lips as a sign of love or affection. 2. to touch gently (a person or thing): A light wind kissed the tulips.*—vi. 1. to give a caress with or as if with the lips, as with pool balls.—n. 1. a caress with the lips, often with suction and pressure. 2. a fancy cake made of powdered sugar and beaten egg whites. 3. a candy containing nuts and coconut.*

I didn't know the word "kiss" had so many meanings. I finger the definition "caress with the lips." That's what Colin did to me. I haven't seen him since he got back from Massachusetts; Harry had tons of work for him.

But maybe sometime in the next month I'll see him. At last week's lesson, Diana said she had more fences for Dove, *Colin* and me to paint. Maybe I'll get a chance to be alone with Colin. I want him to kiss me again.

Every morning, Tess kisses me. Sometimes, she uses so much pressure she knocks me over. She lets me groom her now. I can brush her just about everywhere because she's getting fatter and so brushing doesn't hurt. She lifts each of her hooves in turn for me to clean. When I call her, she comes galloping to me. We're communicating pretty well—at least when I'm not on her.

At yesterday's lesson, Diana said, "You and Tess haven't made the progress I'd hoped for by now."

I was surprised. "But we've made progress," I said. "I understand Tess and me better. When she takes off, I get nervous and I bounce. This makes Tess nervous. She goes faster and then, we kind of bounce apart. We just need to calm ourselves. We're working on that."

"This didn't happen with you and Sweets." Diana said the words gently. She knew they'd hurt.

"Sweets is a nice everyday kind of horse. Tess is, well, she's different." I leaned over in the saddle and wrapped my arms around Tess's sweaty neck. She swung her head around and nuzzled my arm. "A month ago Tess would have been too nervous to nuzzle me while I was on her," I said.

"That's small progress for one month, Willo. . . . Look, there's nothing wrong with admitting you've made a mistake." Diana put her hand on my knee to soften her next words. "We could find a good home for Tess. Then you could start over. With a more suitable horse."

"No!" How could Diana even think of it? "Once you make a commitment to someone or something, you stand by it. That's what my mom always said!"

Diana gave me a funny look. "All right, Willo." She sighed and squeezed my knee. "Next week, we'll try another tactic."

"We will?" I said. She nodded.

"You're not giving up on us?"

"No. I'd never do that."

I wanted to leap off Tess right then and there and hug Diana. She wasn't giving up on us. I knew she wouldn't. Deep inside I knew. She was so much like my mom.

Willo likes—that's what Mom wrote at the top of the typed recipe card I'm now using. Along the border, she added comments: *Use one can tomato paste, not two. Add tablespoon of sugar to sweeten. Roger likes this sweet.* The card's stained with oil and tomato paste.

I toss a small handful of oregano into the pan of hamburger I'm frying. I add a dash of salt, a pinch of dried basil and several shakes of pepper. A worried Boswell eyes me from the top of the refrigerator.

"Don't worry, Bozzie. I know what I'm doing. I've made marzetti before." I study the shelf of spices above the stove. There are so many interesting ones I'd like to try: marjoram, curry powder, coriander, dill, anise . . . I fight the urge to use them all and only add two—marjoram and cayenne pepper, because Granddad likes his marzetti spicy hot.

A timer beeps. I take the noodles I've been boiling and slowly pour them out into a black colander, which I've placed in the sink. Steam rises from the pile of noodles. I turn cold water on them to stop the cooking process, because that's what Mom always did.

Once the hamburger's browned, I add tomato paste—just one can—and cream of tomato soup. I dump in a handful of sugar as rain blows through the kitchen window and the phone rings.

It's Dad. I've barely spoken to him since he's been gone. When I do, I usually say, "Hi. Tess and I are doing fine. Here's Granddad."

"Granddad's at a poker game," I tell Dad now.

"I wanted to speak to you in private," he says, and my heartbeat quickens. Something must be coming. Something's wrong. "August twenty-fifth is your granddad's seventieth birthday," Dad says. "I want him to have a party. Could you help me plan it? Since I can't be there, would you stand in for me?"

"Sure." This isn't what I expected.

"I'll call Josefa. See if she can help. We'll invite your granddad's poker buddies and their wives. We'll invite your gram. I'll order a cake," Dad says. "I've already commissioned a special gift to be made for him."

"What is it?"

"A secret," he says, and I absolutely love the way he says "secret." His voice is warm and just a little mysterious. He's sober. "I'll forward the gift to you. You can give it to him at the party."

"Sure," I say, and he says, "I'm sorry I can't be there."

"Me, too. I wish you could be here now. I'm fixing dinner—marzetti!"

"I didn't know you could cook."

"I can cook marzetti, toast, hamburgers, bacon and chocolate chip cookies.

"How's the Stealth Intruder?" I ask, and I really want to know. I'd like to know everything about Dad right now. He's being nice.

"It's coming slowly," he says. "How's the horse?"

"Coming slowly, too." I don't tell him what Diana said.

"All good things take time," Dad says, which really

surprises me. It's so unlike him. "Remember our poem," he says.

" 'The Darkling Thrush.' I thought of it last week."

"The poem's about hope," Dad says. "No matter how bleak things may be, there's always hope. For growth and change. For happiness. Don't forget that. Promise me?"

"I promise." If I had three wishes, all three would be for Dad to stay like this forever and ever. "I love you, Dad."

"I love you, too," he says.

At night, I sprawl on my bed and look through old family photographs. The last time I looked through them was with Mom. "See this tall lanky guy?" She held up the photo of Dad I'm holding now. He's wearing shorts and T-shirt and he's standing on a beach. "The first time I saw your father, he looked like this. He shaded his eyes as he watched me gallop Swabo along the sand.

"I saw him again a week later at the library where I worked. I was at the reference desk reading book reviews and this warm voice said, 'Could you help me? I need a book on Scotland.'

"I'd been dating two other men at the time, but when I looked up and saw this tall man in his khaki uniform—he was in the Navy then, a first lieutenant— I knew. *This is it. This is the one for me.* It was his eyes.

They were the color of the Pacific Ocean—an intense grayish blue. I've always loved the Pacific. It's unpredictable and full of surprises."

"Like ice cream at midnight?" I said, and Mom had laughed. Every so often, before she got sick, Dad would surprise us by waking us up at midnight. He'd pile us into his car and drive us through darkened streets to an ice cream parlor that stayed open all night long.

Dad is like the Pacific. Sometimes he can be so nice; other times, the drunken times, so mean. He gets me all mixed up inside. I kiss his photo, then stick it underneath my pillow. I hug that pillow. I rock the way I do when I am feeling lonely. I can't give up on Dad. We'll work things out. Somehow we will. I rock and rock, until I rock myself to sleep. And sleeping, I dream I am a photographer. I take pictures of happy families—with two parents and at least one kid. They wear PJs and they all eat ice cream, their intense eyes blazing at my camera.

CHAPTER
14

White fences loom out of an early-morning mist. Counting Saturday when I made marzetti, we've had three days of rain. But now as I walk up Malvern Road toward Diana's house, the sun's coming out. Doves are cooing. I hear mourning doves and the muffled thunder of galloping hooves.

Fingers of mist rise off Diana's front field, a rich deep green. And now, out of the mist, comes Sultan. He gallops downhill toward me. He looks so wild and strong and free! Beyond his barreled chest, his high-flying hooves, tasseled cornstalks rise toward the sky, their green husks full to bursting.

"Hey Sultan!" I call.

Whack! What was that? What made that sound?

Sultan slides to a stop a few yards away from me. Nostrils flared, he stares at me across the fence. His dark eyes are rimmed with white. He's frightened. He half rears.

Whack.

Sultan wheels. He tears off. One moment, I see him. The next, he's disappeared into mist. Hugging myself, I walk slowly uphill, all the time searching for what made those whacks. To warn whoever or whatever could be making them—*I'm in the area; don't whack me*—as I walk, I sing:

> *This old man, he played one,*
> *He played knick-knack on my thumb,*
> *With a knick-knack patty-whack—*

It's just a little nursery song, but it seems to work. There are no more whacks. I jog across Diana's yard and I see the front door slowly closing. There's something dark on the porch—a golf bag propped against a pillar. Probably Jack's. He's the only one who golfs around here. I stop. Was he using the front field for golfing? *Was he knocking golf balls*—whack—*into the field?* No. He wouldn't do that. Would he? But it's so dangerous. Horses graze in that field.

In the stable, I hear voices coming from the tack

room, low and urgent-sounding. Dove's voice. Colin's. *He's in there.* Taking a deep breath, I open the door and there he is, sitting on a trunk, stirring a can of paint held between his knees.

"Hi." My voice cracks. Colin looks up at me and he says nothing. He looks upset. Should I tell him what I just heard and saw? There were these whacks. A golf bag . . . "Where's your mom?" I end up saying.

"At the grocery store," he says, and I say, "Oh."

"There's no milk in the house," Colin says in a flat voice. "Jack told Mom she'd better get some. He wants milk for his cereal and coffee."

"Why doesn't he go out and get it himself?" I say.

"He doesn't do that kind of thing," Colin says.

I know the kind of thing he does, I think, but I don't say this. I didn't actually *see* Jack hit golf balls into the field where Sultan grazed.

"Hey Willo." Dove, holding three paintbrushes, comes out from the large closet where Diana stores supplies. Dove hands me a brush and she gives one to Colin.

"You know," I say to Colin, "once we paint all your fences and get this place fixed up, you could come over to mine. You could help Dove, Granddad, Dad and me cover Mas-Que Farm with Christmas trees. We're going to plant several thousand of them come spring."

Colin says, "If I'm around, I'll help."

"What do you mean—if you're around? Of course you'll be around!" It can't be otherwise.

"You'd like planting trees," Dove says as Colin stirs paint—swirling threads of gold through globs of white. "I helped last spring. We dug holes. We poured in water. We stuck these tiny roots into mud. Willo's dad sang Christmas carols. He made up songs—"

> East is east and west is west
> But the farm's the place for me.
> You can touch the stars with a fishing pole,
> And plant Christmas with a tree.

"Remember that, Willo?"

"I remember." That had been a happy time with Dad.

"Willo's dad loves Christmas trees," Dove says to Colin. "He says their roots reach deep and their limbs soar up to heaven. He said, 'When you plant trees, make certain to give each one plenty of water. Trees need lots of water.' He must have said that a dozen times."

"He got that from my mom," I say, and Colin's eyes meet mine. Does he remember my talking about Mom? She had a Christmas tree in her room. She was always after me to water it. She could only whisper.

"Colin!" A harsh voice shouts from outside the stable. It's Jack. "Colin! Did you mess with my appointment book? Get up here!"

Colin takes a deep breath, whispers something to himself and gets to his feet. He gives Dove and me a sort of half-smile, as if he's apologizing for something. "Go ahead. Start painting without me. I'll join you later if I can."

I am so disappointed. I wanted Colin to join us now. In the front field, Dove and I start sanding a section of fence that's near the stable. We hear Jack's pickup move down the driveway. We see it turn onto Malvern Road. Is Colin with Jack? We don't know. The sun burns off the morning mist, and as it does, Sultan slowly grazes his way over to us. The large horse, who earlier looked so wild, gently takes a carrot I offer him—his muzzle soft against my palm.

"Oh, Willo. Look." Dove draws in her breath and points to a large welt on Sultan's rump.

"Oh my God." I tell Dove about Jack. "You don't think he'd whack golf balls at Sultan, do you? No one could be that mean."

"Maybe Sultan was bitten by a horsefly. Maybe he was stung." I can tell by Dove's tone that she doesn't believe this. She runs her hand along Sultan's neck, down his back and toward the welt. Before Dove can inspect it closely, Sultan wheels and trots away.

As I feel Tess, she feels me. She slows to a collected canter I can sit to. Wow. I could sit to this for hours. I didn't know she could canter like this. I don't want her ever to stop. We canter round and round Diana.

"All right, Willo," she says. "Now we'll walk. Walk, Tess."

"Walk, Tess," I echo, and when she does I pet her lathered neck. "You're so good. You're such a good horse."

"She certainly is," Diana says. "And you, Willo, are one very special rider."

CHAPTER
16

I'm sandwiched between Colin and Diana as we gallop Sultan along a beach. My arms are wrapped around Diana and my cheek's pressed against her back. I feel so content. I can smell her perfume. It reminds me of some kind of incense—the exotic kind that's made in India, where women have beautiful dark eyes and red circles on their foreheads.

Colin sits behind me. Colin holds me in his arms. Oh. I feel his breath against my neck. Diana turns Sultan into the ocean, his dark hooves splashing water. I feel water on my bare feet and warm lips on my neck. Colin's kissing my neck and I feel as if I am on fire. A wave curls, about to crash down on our heads. A ringing wave. It rings and rings. The phone. The phone?

I find myself in bed. No Colin. No Diana. I'm so disappointed, I want to cry. The phone rings on and on. I stumble across the hall. "Hello?"

"Willo. I've been thinking about school," Dad says. He woke me up from the grandest dream to talk about school? It's not even the end of August! I glance at the clock. It's three A.M.

"You need school clothes." Dad says each word too precisely. I feel like throwing up.

"I have clothes from last year," I manage to say.

"You have clothes." He says this like it's some kind of miracle. "And classes?" he says. "What classes are you taking?"

"You know. You said I had to take Algebra Two and honors history."

"You like history," he says. "And English. You're taking English."

"Yessir."

"Right then. You're set. Good night, Willo."

"Good night." I slam down the phone and stumble back to bed. I want to return to my dream. I want the dream to go on and on and never end. But the dream

I fall into is planting Christmas trees with Dad. In new school clothes, I stand over him while he packs mud around a Scotch pine's tiny roots. He's smiling up at me.

I draw close and that's when I smell whiskey on his breath. He holds out his arms to me and I back away. I run—disappearing into mist. The next morning, I wake up feeling all discombobulated. *He's drinking.* I don't want to get out of bed. But it's Josefa's day to clean. Dove has caught a ride with her grandmother to the farm and now Dove's pouncing on my bed. "Come on, Willo." She shakes my shoulders. "Let's go riding!"

In the tack room, it's cool, but not as cool as the ocean I dreamed about last night. A breeze coming through the windows makes cobwebs above the feed bins dance like white foam on ocean waves. Dove's been telling me about her cat, Celeste. "She escaped from the house two days ago," Dove says. "She was in heat and now she's not. Grandma Josefa says she's pregnant."

"I don't think it can happen that fast." I grab Tess's saddle and bridle and shoulder open the tack room door. I stop dead. Maybe things can happen fast. Cats get pregnant. Things get started in a dream—

It's Colin and he's on Sultan. The large dark horse

fills the barn's open doorway. I've never seen Colin on Diana's horse—except in dreams. Colin looks taller on Sultan than he did on Cloudy. His hair curls out from beneath his hard hat. He looks a little wild—in a black shirt and ripped jeans. Sultan paws the ground. The tip of his horseshoe catches the edge of the barn's concrete floor—*clink*.

"Oh my goodness," Dove says from behind me. And then, to Colin, "You rode Sultan the whole way here?"

"Well, we didn't fly." Colin grins.

"You're both all muddy," Dove says. Sultan's belly, legs and flanks are covered with mud. As are Colin's boots. I hadn't noticed.

"We got caught up in a little swamp." Colin says this so casually, as if a little swamp is nothing. But if that little swamp was the Confederates' Swamp, it's something. A great big something. There's quicksand back there. "Where are you two riding?"

"Willo's ring." Dove knows the ring is the only place I am allowed to ride. I'm itching to break out of it. At my last riding lesson, Tess and I communicated— off the lunge line. We were in sync. Diana was pleased. "Want to ride with us?" Dove asks Colin.

Say yes, Colin. He looks at me and he says, "Sure."

There's no way I'm going to lead Tess to the ring

and back with Colin here. In the barnyard, I ask Dove to hold Tess still for me so that I can mount. Dove looks surprised. She knows Dad's order: *You're not to ride Tess anywhere but in the ring.* But I'm only going to ride Tess to the ring and back. It's no big deal; we're ready. I swing up on Tess. Sultan draws near. He's a hand taller than Tess and maybe two times heavier. When they sniff noses, she trembles.

As we head uphill toward Granddad's house, Colin jogs Sultan on one side of my prancing Tess and Dove jogs Toby on the other. "What happened in the swamp?" I ask Colin.

"He got caught up in some vines. He spooked."

"We'll have to clean those vines out." I glance at Colin. He's looking at me. He has dark circles under his eyes. Hasn't he been sleeping? I don't think his mom's been sleeping. At last week's lesson, Diana's eyes looked so huge and dark. But maybe it was her hair that made them look that way. She'd just had her hair cut really short. "I needed a change," she told me. "Jack and Colin don't like it. What do you think?"

I said it made her look pretty, and it did!

As we round the old pump house at the edge of Granddad's yard, Sultan sidles into Tess. She, in turn, bumps into Toby. My stirrup bangs against Dove's knee. "Sorry, Dove."

"It's okay." She guides Toby over to the side of the road. Tess, uneasy with Sultan, follows Toby. She frets, tossing froth on Toby's neck. She jerks at the bit. I feel my stomach tighten. *Relax.*

Far ahead of us, Granddad's car turns off the highway and onto Mas-Que's driveway. If I can see him, he can see me—on Tess. Outside the ring. *It's no big deal.* I'll talk to Granddad about it later.

We turn into the sheep's pasture and Sultan plunges forward, breaking into a canter. He passes Tess and she leans on the bit. She wants to take off after him. I tighten the reins. *Don't run away.* I grab hold of an imagined rope and, thinking of Diana, I sit deep.

Sultan's churning hooves kick up sod. Neck arched, body drawn into itself and ready to explode, Sultan throws his head, trying to get the bit between his teeth. Colin rises in the stirrups. He saws on Sultan's reins. Will Sultan get away from him?

No. Colin may not know how to get along with his mom's husband, but his hands sure know how to play her horse. I watch how his hands move—give a little, take a little. He settles back into the saddle. He brings Sultan to a collected canter so beautiful and slow Tess can prance to it.

Sultan, dark to begin with, grows darker with sweat. The reins, rubbing against his neck, work up a lather. He leans lightly against the bit. *He's on the bit.* Colin canters him past the Christmas trees. Sunlight gleams off Colin's hands and that lather, white against Sultan's neck. It's the most beautiful sight I've ever seen.

CHAPTER
17

There is a water stain on the ceiling above Granddad's head. The giant stain is shaped like a hand with
four fingers and a thumb, and its grasp is wider than
Granddad's desk. Mom called this stain "the hand of
God." When she was in pain, she'd imagine the hand
holding her. "It's warm," she told me. "When I lay my
cheek against its palm, I can feel God's heartbeat and
I am not afraid."

Mom left us in December and the hand of God re-
mains. I stand in the doorway to Granddad's office—
a place I hardly ever go because Mom died in here. I

hold up a horse book she'd given me. "Guess what this says?"

Granddad, with Christmas tree brochures spread out on the desk before him, peers at me over the rims of his reading glasses.

"This horse book, recommended by the American Horse Show Association, says it's important to have fun with riding. If all you do is work, work, work, neither you nor your horse will enjoy it. You'll grow ring-sour. You'll burn out!

"You need to take a break. Go on trail rides and play. Life should be balanced between work and play."

Granddad takes off his glasses and rubs his eyes. "Willojean. Why are you quoting this book to me?"

"Because it's important that you know these things."

"Why's that?"

"Because today you saw me riding Tess outside the ring."

"I did?"

"Didn't you?"

"Why don't you tell me about it?"

"I rode Tess with Dove and Colin to the ring and back. That was all." I take a deep breath and let it out. "We were ready for it, Granddad. We're doing well. We're making progress. Diana says so.

"Tess doesn't get so upset at being left behind. She's

getting smarter. She knows there's more to life than racing."

"Of course there is. There's Willojean." Granddad's eyes look into mine. He doesn't grin or anything. He's serious. He means this. A sudden shaft of sunlight catches the hand of God above him. And oh, that hand is glowing.

"I have no problem with your riding Tess outside the ring," Granddad says. "But I'm not the commanding officer. You'll need to check this with your dad."

"Yessir! I'll call him about it tonight."

At ten P.M., which is seven P.M. California time, I sit at Dad's desk with the green blotter. No letters are lined up on it now because Granddad forwards all Dad's mail to California. No laundry is piled up on Dad's bed. The room feels empty. Outside the window in front of the desk, the sky is dark.

With trembling hands, I call Dad's apartment. The phone rings and rings. He must not be home. I hope he's not out drinking. I'm about to hang up when the phone clicks and a voice says, "Hello."

"Dad?"

"No. It's Alex. I'll get Roger for you. It's Roger you want, right? Not Tom, Jonathan or David?"

"It's Roger."

The man puts the phone down and music blasts

into it. I hear rock music, men's voices and the hated sound of ice being poured into a glass. Someone shouts, "Roger. Sounds like it's a daughter on the phone. You never told me you had a daughter."

There's mumbling and then Dad's voice. "Willo?"

"Hi Dad. Sounds as if you're having a party. That must be fun."

"Fun?" He calls out, "Alex, would you call what we're doing fun?"

There's the sound of laughter and Dad says, "I wouldn't call this fun, Willo. My team's just taking a break from an eighty-hour work week."

"It's important to take breaks." I want to build up naturally to the one I took—riding to and from the ring. "How's work?"

"Work needs minor adjustments."

"Here's to minor adjustments!" a voice calls out from Dad's end of the line.

Dad says, "I'll drink to that."

I stare out the window. All I see is the huge black night. I want to take the phone I'm holding and throw it at the night. I want Dad to hear the sound of breaking glass.

"Work needs minor adjustments," Dad repeats. "That, of course, and by definition, means major ones. In our business, there is nothing minor. Right, Alex?"

There is laughter.

"I'm not Alex," I whisper. I clear my throat. "Dad, I wanted to ask you about—"

"Alex," Dad says, "give David some of that scotch."

"Dad? I rode Tess outside the—"

"For God's sake, Alex, give David the scotch!"

"I just rode her—"

"Not the bourbon, Alex!"

Downstairs, Granddad's watching TV. I hear firing guns and shouting voices. I want to add to that the sound of breaking window glass, but this is Granddad's house and I don't want to hurt it. Dad's yelling for some guy called Jonathan now. I slam the phone down, hard.

In the living room Granddad says to me, "Did you talk to our C.O.?"

"Yessir, I did."

"And what did he say?"

"He says whatever I want to do with Tess is fine with him. I can ride her where I please." I cross my fingers to counter the lie. If it really is a lie. The way Dad acted on the phone, for him I didn't exist. If I don't exist, I'm not a member of his command and he can't issue orders to me. I'm free.

CHAPTER
18

Tess trembles beneath me as she watches Granddad escort Gram over to the ring to see us. Gram's all dressed up for Granddad's birthday party. She looks pretty in her purple dress and big straw hat with pink flowers that the breeze keeps trying to steal away. Giggling, she clutches the flapping hat with one hand while holding on to Granddad's arm with the other. They look good together—Dad's mom and Mom's dad. If Gram wasn't so set on living in her little house on the Eastern Shore, she and Granddad could get married. They could be my parents.

I urge Tess over to the gate to greet my Gram. She

has on pink lipstick that matches the flowers in her hat, and even from on high, I can smell her perfume. She smells like lilacs.

"Hi Gram," I say, and she says, "Hi yourself! And what do we have here?"

"This is Tess."

"Well, hello, Tess." Gram reaches into her dress pocket and brings out a sugar cube. "I've never fed a horse before," she says to Granddad.

"I'll help you." He flattens Gram's hand and puts the sugar cube in her palm. He supports the back of Gram's hand as she holds it up. Tess takes the treat they offer and then stretches out her head to nibble at Gram's hat.

"No, Tess! You can't have that." Gram places her hand on Tess's muzzle. Tess nuzzles her and Gram chuckles. She chuckles the same way Dad does when he's in a good mood—low and funny-sounding.

"What do you think of my horse?" My voice sounds high-pitched and tense. I clear my throat and bury my knuckles in Tess's mane.

"She's sprickety." Gram smiles, so sprickety must be all right. Gram feeds Tess a second sugar cube. This time by herself. "Eat it up. Eat every bite. We need to fatten you up, sweet thing." Tears glisten in Gram's eyes.

"What's wrong, Gram?"

"She's all skin and bones, Willo."

"Skin and bones?" I'm surprised. I've grown so used to Tess I don't think of her as skinny anymore. I see my mare as proud, frisky and sometimes a little wild. "Don't worry, Gram. I'll fatten her up."

"That's my Willo." With a little white handkerchief, she dabs her eyes. "You're a good girl. So kind. Just like your mother." Gram smiles up at Granddad and he hugs her. I feel all tight inside. Mom's gone. Dad might as well be. Tess starts to fidget and I tell myself, *Relax.*

We hold Granddad's party out on the screened-in porch off the living room. The porch is the one room that's large enough for Granddad's seven poker buddies and their wives. Granddad looks flushed and happy in the light from the eight candles Josefa and I put on his chocolate cake. The light makes Granddad look young, which, turned around in my head, makes me realize he's growing old.

"Eight candles?" he asks me.

"One for each ten years of your life, plus one to grow on."

"That makes me seven years old and growing." Granddad looks from one grinning person to the next. His eyes light up when they meet Gram's. She sits in a white wicker rocking chair and the wind plays with the flowers in her hat.

Granddad puffs his cheeks to blow out the candles. "Don't forget to make a wish!" I say. Granddad nods. He pauses, then blows out every candle. All in one breath! Everybody cheers.

I help Josefa serve the cake and ice cream while downhill, in a rising wind, the shrouds on Dad's sailboat go *clinkety-clink, clinkety-clink*. The *Bonnie Prince* needs to leave its mooring and go for a good long sail. It needs to play, the way I've been doing on Tess these past two days. We've rambled through the fields and down to the creek. Tess loves this rambling and so do I.

After cake and ice cream, Granddad gets up to speak. He clears his throat, thanks everyone for coming and then starts talking about Mas-Que—"that sorry excuse for a farm" his poker buddies told him not to buy.

"Well, I can tell you, the years spent working Mas-Que have been some of the best ones in my life," Granddad says, and I sit up. Oh, I grow still and silent. Often, when people start talking about the best years, they're going to announce the end of something.

"They haven't been easy years," Granddad says, "but by God, they've been rich. However, a few years back, I began to think that tending the farm was getting beyond the capabilities of an old sea dog like me."

"No, Granddad!" The words come out of me before I can stop them.

He says, "Willojean. Come here."

I want the wind to gust. Blow napkins, paper plates and cake crumbs all over and create a slight diversion, because everyone's looking at me. Once I get to Granddad, I snuggle myself beneath his arm.

He says, "This summer, Willo's been playing a tough hand—working with a high-strung thoroughbred ex-racehorse. It hasn't been easy, has it, Willo?"

"No, sir."

"Seven weeks ago, she dumped you in the manure pile. You got a little dirty. Maybe a little scared. But that didn't stop you from getting back on. You're stubborn—a bit like me. And a whole lot like your mother." Granddad looks at me, his sea-blue eyes so bright and shining. This is the second time today I've been compared to Mom. If I'm so like her, how could Dad forget me?

"A few years ago, I sold off my livestock," Granddad says softly. "I quit growing corn and tobacco. I didn't plant soybeans. I spent most of my day watching TV. That's when my daughter, Mary, came to me with a dream of covering the farm with Christmas trees.

"Each time I mentioned retiring, Mary talked about Scotch pines and blue spruce. She said I should plant Douglas fir in Mas-Que's swampy areas and white pine in the front field. On my sixty-ninth birthday, she presented me with a planting mattock and pruning shears.

"What does one do in the face of such determination?" Granddad says.

"One plants Christmas trees," I whisper. My throat aches. I feel as if Mom is all around me. In the wind playing with Gram's hat. In the talk of trees . . .

"That's right." Granddad tousles my hair and I lean into him. "This past spring we planted a thousand trees. Next spring—my seventieth spring—we'll plant ten thousand more. By the time I'm eighty, you, my friends, will have Mas-Que Farm Christmas trees in your living rooms."

"Here's to Ike Murdock and his Christmas trees!" Red Condon, who owns the farm across the creek from ours, lifts a glass of punch and he toasts Granddad. Gram, in a high quivery voice, starts to sing: "O Christmas tree, O Christmas tree, how lovely are thy branches." One by one, we all join in. It all feels so solemn and beautiful.

When the song is done, I give Granddad a long rectangular box—the secret gift Dad sent from California. I have no idea what's in the heavy box and I have told myself that I don't care.

"Well, let's see what my son-in-law has sent." What Granddad pulls out from the box brings tears to his eyes. It's the perfect gift. Mom would have loved it—a redwood sign, and on it are stamped the words

MAS-QUE FARM
CHRISTMAS TREE PLANTATION.

When Granddad reads aloud the card that Dad has sent, I feel all mixed up; I want to cry. The card says, *Happy Seventieth Birthday! And here's to Christmas Trees! With love and gratitude for all you've done to keep our family together—Roger and Willojean.*

CHAPTER
19

School starts in September and the hours I'd like to spend with Tess are taken up with algebra, English, French, music, art and honors history. I wish school offered a course on training a horse. I could use that.

I'm sketching a horse in my history notebook when my history teacher, Dr. Atwell, says, "The word 'deadline' comes from the Civil War." *That's interesting.* I stop sketching and close the notebook. "Andersonville and other Civil War prison camps had prison yards with a twelve-foot-high outer pine-board fence," Dr. Atwell says. "Inside this was a smaller fence or ditch. Three feet inside this was the deadline—so called because the guards would shoot dead, without warning, any prisoner caught stepping over it.

"It's come to mean a line or boundary that must not be crossed," Dr. Atwell says. "So, class. When I give a deadline for your papers, keep it." Looking over his glasses, he winks at us.

Beneath my desk, I jiggle my feet. I've been given a November 2 deadline for Tess. By then, I need to prove to Dad that she and I belong together. We're a pair. I want Tess to jump! That will show Dad—with this horse I can do anything.

But can I? At last week's lesson, Diana started Tess and me on the first phase of jumping—trotting over cavalletti. As we headed toward the set of five poles placed a stride apart along the ground, I rose in my stirrups. I kept my eyes up and heels down. *Three more strides. Here we go.*

Tess ducked out on me and there I went. On the ground. My frightened horse trotted around the ring—reins and stirrups flapping.

"You let her duck out on you," Diana said. "Next time, keep your outside rein taut and push her forward."

It took three more tries before I could get Tess to trot over the poles. Even then, she did it sideways like a crab. If only I could get her on the bit, I bet I could make her face those poles head-on.

Outside Dr. Atwell's classroom, a flock of geese cuts through the gray and windy sky, honking wildly. The maple trees that line the soccer field are starting to turn red. On the blackboard, Dr. Atwell writes the word "deadline." This Sunday, after Granddad talked with Dad, he said, "I don't like what his deadline's doing to him. He's all keyed up—"

He's drinking.

It's September 28. Dad has five weeks to make his deadline for the Stealth Intruder. I have five weeks to train Tess. A leaf—a red leaf—swirls in the center of the soccer field. It swirls round and round, going nowhere but in circles. Dad and I haven't really spoken to each other since the day I slammed down the phone. We just act polite and say, "Hello. How are you?" There's always an awkward silence that makes my insides ache.

The wind coming through Granddad's car window smells of cut hay and apples. The sun hangs low. Below it stretches acre upon acre of corn, waiting to be harvested. Granddad drives us past horse farms and through a little village. He turns onto a winding road that leads uphill.

Granddad's driving me to the first fall meeting of the Tidewater Pony Club. Usually meetings are held at Diana's house. But tonight, the Bit and Spur Pony Club has invited us to a special presentation given by Dr. Beidleman, "The Diseases of the Horse," at St. Francis of Assisi Roman Catholic Church.

The church has pretty stained-glass windows that are lit up by a light within. A cross, high on the steeple, casts a shadow across a graveyard. I can't remember whether Mom's grave, way up north in a family burial plot in New York State, has a church beside it. It would be nice.

The crowded meeting room is dark and noisy. I search the rows of seated kids for Dove and Colin. I haven't seen Colin since he rode to the farm on Sultan. His high school is five miles from the middle school Dove and I attend. There's Dove.

"Where's Colin?" I ask, slipping into the seat beside her.

"On the Eastern Shore. With Jack. They're repairing a broken duck blind. Jack's making Colin go duck hunting with him this fall."

"Does Colin like to hunt ducks?"

"He hates it. The duck blind's small and crowded. Jack drinks whiskey to stay warm and he shoots everything in sight."

I feel chilled. "Colin shouldn't hunt with Jack."

"If things go as Colin's planned, he won't."

"What do you mean by that?"

"I can't say."

"But—"

"Leave it, Willo." Dove stares at the projector screen. I know not to press her; Dove's loyal. She keeps secrets. Still—

Dr. Beidleman clears his throat. The slide projector clicks on. The picture on the screen startles me. It's of torn flesh. Blood. A wounded horse. His shoulder's gashed.

"That's gross!" a girl behind me says.

"To a veterinarian," Dr. Beidleman says, "the wound is beautiful. Because it holds the possibility, the hope of being healed."

I've never thought of a wound this way. Wounds are ugly. They cause pain. A second slide flashes on. Needle in hand, Dr. Beidleman is sewing up the gash. The third slide shows the wound up close—stitches black against a golden coat.

"Here he is six months later." Dr. Beidleman clicks the projector, and the horse with the gash—a chestnut quarter horse—gallops across a green field, his tail held high and happy.

Dr. Beidleman's presentation is full of sick or injured horses. Some just can't be healed; most can. He shows slides of a mare giving birth. I have trouble looking at these. They make me feel queasy. Not Dove. When the foal is finally born, she says, "I want to be a veterinarian when I grow up."

I can see why Dove would want to be a vet. Healing is a wonderful thing—making the world well. Dove could do it. She's Catholic. She goes to Holy Masses and she knows priests. But it's not for me. I couldn't face my mom's sickness. I hated to see her in pain. I don't want anything to do with blood, pain, being born or dying. Unless it comes to Tess. For Tess, I will face anything.

After Dr. Beidleman's presentation, Diana gets up to speak. In the overhead light, her skin takes on a strange glow—like something hot is burning inside her. Is she worried about Colin? *He'll be all right.*

"This November, someone special is visiting my farm," she says. "Ted Walliker. You may have heard of him. He's an outstanding horseman. An expert on jumping."

He is? I feel my heartbeat quicken.

"He's agreed to give a jumping clinic for both pony clubs at my place." Diana looks at me as she is saying this.

You want me to come? Of course I'll come! I want to jump! But why aren't you giving the clinic yourself?

"Ted lives in Maryland," Diana says, "but he's trained champion jumpers from as far away as California. He really is the best. On Friday night, November second, he'll show a video highlighting his training techniques. On Saturday, you'll get a hands-on chance to work with Ted—he's giving classes on the flat and over fences."

November 2?

"We'll go to the Friday night thing together," Dove whispers to me as I stare at Diana. Why November 2? Why not October 19? The twenty-sixth? Any other date? "I'll spend the night at your house," Dove is saying. "That way, we can be together. We'll get up early. We'll groom the horses—"

"Sure, Dove," I say, my stomach twisting. Dad never gave me permission to ride Tess outside the ring, and here I'll be, riding her at Diana's the weekend he gets home. But how can I give up the clinic? Ted's an expert. He's trained champions.

CHAPTER
20

The smell of frying onions, garlic and chili peppers comes from Josefa's kitchen. She's in there talking to herself in Spanish as she cooks *tacos de machaca* for Colin, Dove and me because, she says, it will give us strength for riding horses. We are all too skinny.

I sit on her orange, yellow and tan braided rug while above me on the sofa, Dove French-braids my hair. Across from us, Colin strums guitar and sings a song he made up about the wind. It's a crazy song, full of nonsense words. As he sings, an October wind blows rain against the windows and makes the inside of Josefa's apartment feel cozy. It's attached to Dove's house, but you wouldn't know it. The small apartment feels like a world apart. It's decorated in shades of white and blue and green with splashes of red and orange. And flowers. Josefa has flowers everywhere. Plastic flowers. Cloth flowers. She has a cross hanging in the hall and that has fresh flowers under it—marigolds. Yellow and orange marigolds.

When he finishes singing, Colin sits back in his chair, the guitar straddling his lap. Absentmindedly, he plucks the strings. Colin has long fingers like his mom's. I love those fingers. "Are you two riding in the East Wind Horse Show?" he asks.

"I'm going to," Dove says.

"Not me. Tess isn't ready." I can get her to trot over cavalletti smoothly now, but she sometimes does it sideways. When she gets keyed up, I have trouble stopping her. And we haven't learned to jump. When I go to a horse show, I want to jump. "Will you be riding Sultan in it?" I ask.

"Mom's not sure I should. He's always been a little wild. Lately, he's gone crazy-wild." Colin looks over my head and says to Dove, "Jack's been teasing him again."

He has?

Dove's hands, which have been braiding my hair, grow suddenly still. Something butts against my arm. Celeste. Dove's calico cat climbs into my lap. She puts her paws on my chest and rubs her chin against my cheek. Her stomach bulges with kittens. Things happen so fast. Cats get pregnant. Horses get teased. They go crazy-wild . . .

"When does duck hunting season begin?" Dove asks Colin over my head. I wish she wouldn't do this; it sets me apart from them.

"It's already started," Colin says. "Don't worry. Mom and I have made arrangements. We've worked things out."

Arrangements? What's he talking about? I look at Dove. She bites her lip: *Sorry. Can't go into this.* She turns my head around. I feel her fingers on my scalp as she resumes gathering bits of hair and weaving it into one long braid. Sometimes I wish I knew Colin the way she does. He nestles his guitar under his arm and says, "This song's for you, Willo."

> *The water is wide, I cannot get over,*
> *And neither have I the wings to fly.*
> *Give me a boat that can carry two,*
> *And both shall row, Willojean and I.*

He's singing this song about him and me? Just the two of us? But the tune he plays is so slow and sad. Is the song about the beginning of something? It sounds as if we might be going on a journey. Oh, I'd go anywhere with Colin. Josefa comes out of the kitchen as he's singing. Wiping her plump hands on her apron, she says, "All right, *mis queridos,* time to eat."

At the small dining room table, Dove sits facing her grandma. I sit across from Colin. Josefa bows her head, so we bow ours. She prays softly in Spanish. Her husband brought her to America forty years ago; she speaks English for everyday things. But she always prays in Spanish. Her Spanish prayers filled Grand-dad's house when my mom was dying.

When she's finished praying, Josefa's warm dark eyes encourage us to finish every bite of her *tacos de machaca.* From a shelf on the wall behind her, the photo of her husband—Dove's Grandpa Ernest, who died two years ago—looks on.

Last year, I visited his grave with Josefa and Dove. It was on All Souls' Day, which Josefa calls *el día de todos los muertos*—the Day of the Dead. According to Josefa, on *el día de todos los muertos,* the souls of the dead are said to come back to visit the living. The living bring the dead their favorite food to eat. They pray for them. They tell the dead that they will never be forgotten.

I wish Mom's grave weren't so far away. Then I could visit it. I'd tell my mom, "You will never be for-gotten." I never even got to tell my mom good-bye. When Dad brought her home from the hospital for the last time, he didn't tell me he was bringing her home to die. He said, "Your mother's going to be just fine."

The first two lines of Colin's song come back to me:

The water is wide, I cannot get over,
And neither have I the wings to fly.

It's such a sad song. Why'd he choose it for us? I look across the table at him. Over a forkful of steaming food, his eyes meet mine. They do not look away. Outside, there is the wind. Outside, there is so much rain. But I feel safe and warm in Josefa's house with its flowers and its steaming food. Colin's here with his red hair. His hazel eyes. That mouth.

Colin? Can I kiss your mouth?

CHAPTER
21

On the day of the East Wind Horse Show, I bury my cold hands in Tess's fuzzy winter coat and trot her up the road toward the grumbling sound of Granddad's tractor. The apples on Granddad's trees have turned bright red. Tess eyes them, her breath steaming the frosty air.

"You'll get one later," I promise.

Nearing Granddad's house, Tess catches sight of Boswell. He suns himself on the large boulder that once streaked through outer space. Tess gathers herself beneath me, ready to explode should Boswell attack. Old Bozzie's green eyes follow Tess as she prances past *his* boulder. *His* yard. Neck arched, tail held high, Tess snorts: *Isn't life exciting?*

It sure is. Life's a roller coaster. One moment you're down, the next you're soaring. I'm soaring. Dad phoned this morning. He sounded happy to speak to me. We really talked for the first time in weeks. He said, "Get on your dancing shoes, Willo. Get out the champagne. My team's made a major breakthrough with the Stealth Intruder. Next Friday, when we present it to the U.S. Navy, the design will knock their socks off."

"You made your deadline?" I said.

"I did. My team did." Dad sounded good to me. Sober and triumphant. "When I come home, we'll celebrate."

"A week from Friday?" That would be November 2.

"No. Can't make it until the fifth," he said apologetically.

That's okay, Dad. I'd learn to jump Tess at the clinic. Dad would come home afterward. We'd celebrate—his victory and mine. And then, I'd show him what Tess and I had learned to do.

"I'm going to be a good father for you, Willo," Dad said. "No more California for me. When I come home this time, I'm staying put. I'm insisting they let me work in Baltimore.

"When I come home, we'll go sailing."

"Sure, Dad." *I haven't sailed with you since last November. There was a northwest wind and Mom, and there were mares' tails in the sky.*

I spy Granddad—mowing grass in the front field beneath a windy sky. I trot Tess over to him and he shuts off the tractor. Eyeing that big red tractor, Tess sidles. I turn her so that she faces the machine. She blows out her nostrils at it. "Is this where we're planting Scotch pines next spring?" I ask.

"From the middle of this field and back." Granddad points in the direction of the house. "We'll plant blue spruce in the silo field. And perhaps in that field behind the barn. You don't use it much."

"No, sir. There's too much farm equipment in it." It's a hilly field with a broken down wagon and a rusty hay rake stored at the downhill end.

"We've got to get that place cleaned out." Granddad gazes at Tess. She paws the ground, eager to move on. "Early this morning, I saw a horse truck come down the driveway."

"It was for Toby. Dove's riding him in the East Wind Horse Show." I can't keep the yearning out of my voice. I would have liked to ride in that horse show, too.

"But you're riding Tess in some important clinic next week," Granddad reminds me.

"Yessir," I say. "A jumping clinic." Granddad understands why I must ride in this clinic. As soon as I told him about it, he'd said I should go.

Granddad straightens himself in the tractor seat, goes to turn the key, then pauses. He looks sideways at me. "Those boots you're wearing. How old are they?"

"I don't know."

"Willojean," he says. "You can't go to a jumping clinic wearing those! They are the oldest and sorriest-looking boots I have ever seen. This afternoon, I'm taking you out to buy new ones. Tall black boots. The most beautiful black boots you've ever seen."

"Oh, Granddad, you're so—"

"You go on now," he says. "Get that mare in shape for the clinic."

"Yessir!" I turn my mare and we trot across the front field to the sheep's pasture. It's a great day. Granddad's buying me boots. Dad's coming home— after the clinic. The sky's bright blue. All the leaves are turning color. The wind sends golden leaves dancing across the field in front of us. I smell ripe apples on the wind. A happy Tess holds her ears so far forward they must hurt.

In the ring, I school her at a walk and trot, now at a canter. I sit deep and everything's so beautiful. The sky. The leaves. My life. Nothing can go wrong. Tess leans lightly on the bit. She puts her weight into my hands. Through the reins I feel her mouth. Through my seat and thighs, I feel the power of her gathered strength.

A playful wind blows against the back of my neck. It sets all the nearby Christmas trees to dancing. I feel connected to my horse in a strange new way. It's as if she's giving everything—all that she is—to me.

Oh my God. This is it.

She's on the bit. After four months of trying, she's on the bit! I move with Tess. She moves with me. I wish Diana were here. I want her to see this. I pet Tess's arched neck. "Dad made his deadline. And know what, Tess? I think we just made ours." *We can jump.*

I've only ever trotted Tess over cavalletti, so the jump I make to celebrate what we've just done is a little one—only two feet high. I make it by propping a pole between a bucket and the fence. But as we approach the jump, it suddenly seems higher. Five feet high!

A few strides away, I feel Tess hesitate.

"We can do this, girl." With my seat and legs I drive her toward the jump. She pulls toward the inside of the ring. I pull her back. We have to face this squarely. *Come on, Tess. One. Two. Three.* She lifts off, thrusting me forward and upward. I grab her mane to keep from pulling on her mouth. I grip hard with my knees. For a moment, we sail—blue sky all around us. Then her front hooves hit ground, my hands braced against her neck.

We recover. We go on. "I love you, Tess," I tell her as we take the jump again. And again. I can't seem to get enough of it. Tess is a natural at this. She's a jumper and so am I. Now all I need to do is prove it to Dad.

"Before you know it, Tess and I will be jumping in the Madison Square Garden Horse Show," I tell Granddad later. "It's the biggest and the best."

"Before you know it, you'll be promoted to fleet admiral and running this place." Granddad hugs me. He's taken a shower after working in the fields and he smells good, spicy and ready for a celebration. We go out for lunch—chocolate milk shakes, hamburgers and french fries. After that, Granddad buys me boots. Tall black boots. Granddad was right. They are the most beautiful boots I have ever seen.

rhythm of her trot. We circle Diana several times and I surprise myself; I begin to feel Tess, thrusting me out of the saddle on one beat, asking me to settle down into it on the next.

We trot round and round and Diana says, "Walk."

"Walk, Tess." I let myself sink into the saddle. Tess drops her head and, for the first time ever, walks for me. Just like that. I'm stunned.

"She's never walked like this before." I try to keep the excitement out of my voice. I don't want Tess to get keyed up again.

"You're relaxed and so is she. Concentrate on that feeling. It's a state you want to aim for in riding Tess. A calm steady rider makes a calm and sensible mount."

We amble around Diana—our control tower. She doesn't look small the way she did the other day. Here, in my ring, Diana is the center of the universe.

"Prepare to canter, Willo," Diana says.

I reach up to grab the reins from Tess's neck.

"No reins, Willo."

Canter without reins? Diana waits for me to sit back. She flicks her whip. "Canter, Tess."

I squeeze Tess with my outside leg and she plunges forward, throwing me up and out of the saddle. I fall onto her neck. I grab her mane, trying to regain my balance as Tess, the supercharged carousel horse, tears around the ring.

"Easy, girl." Her pounding hooves churn up dust. She coughs. I choke. *This is never going to work.* Diana calls out, "Sit back, Willo."

I'm afraid to sit back.

"I'm in control," she says calmly. Firmly. "Nothing can happen. Sit back. Relax."

I sit back. I bounce all over. Tess flattens her ears. She doesn't like this and neither do I.

"Imagine a rope running down through the center of your body," Diana calls out across the ring. "It's anchored to something so solid and deep nothing can dislodge it.

"Grab that rope, Willo."

"I can't grab a rope that I can't see."

"It's there. Believe me. Grab it."

Choking in dust, being tossed up and down, I imagine a rope like the one Diana's holding. In my mind, I grab it.

"Sit deep. Hold the rope and rock. Hold and rock," Diana says while Tess tosses me up and down. We've had three days of hot sunshine and the ring's a sea of dust.

Hold and rock.

Gradually, so gradually I'm not aware of the precise moment, I begin to feel the rhythm of Tess's canter: *Da-da-dump. Da-da-dump.* I begin to move with Tess like a ship moves along the surface of the sea.

CHAPTER
22

Coriander or cumin?" I ask Granddad. I'm at the stove, helping him fix a celebratory dinner of chicken curry. After all, it's not often a girl gets her horse to come on the bit and take a jump in the same day.

"Add a little of both." Granddad surveys the condiments he's set out on the counter. "And a few dashes of hot sauce."

"Yessir!" As I stir the thickening sauce, I keep an eye out for the truck bringing Dove and Toby back from the horse show. I have so much to tell Dove! The truck doesn't come. And doesn't come. It's not until

Granddad and I have each eaten two platefuls of curry and an ice cream cone that that truck finally arrives.

"That was a long show!" I take the saddle and bridle Dove's holding so she can lead Toby down the ramp. Dove's shirttail has come out of her jodhpurs. Her boots are dusty and her cheeks are smudged. Has she been crying?

"What happened? What's wrong?" I ask as we walk Toby to the barn.

"Nothing." She doesn't say anything more, which isn't like Dove. Tess, seeing Toby, whinnies to him: *Where have you been?* Toby drags Dove over to Tess so that she can nuzzle him.

"So. How did you do?" I ask.

"Toby won second place in the pleasure class." Dove leans against the stall door while Tess and Toby nuzzle each other.

"A second place? That's great."

"I guess so." What's wrong with Dove? If I'd won a ribbon in a horse show, I'd be so happy I'd dance all over. "How did Colin do?"

"He won the Jumper Championship on Sultan." Dove looks at me and bursts into tears. "There was a jump-off," she sobs. "The fences were five feet high. Colin was the youngest rider and everyone was cheering. Sultan cleared every fence."

"So why are you crying?"

CHAPTER
15

Even though I kept praying he would, Colin didn't return to help us paint. Diana, back from the store, told Dove and me he had to go with Jack to clean up a construction site. As she spoke, Diana kept looking at her house. She seemed anxious. Even though we wouldn't be finished for hours, she said, "I'll pay you now. Otherwise, I might forget." She smiled, as if apologizing for something. She hugged us both. She touched my cheek.

There was so much I wanted to say to her. *I'm sorry for the fight you had with Jack. Sorry about Sultan. What's going on with Colin? Will Colin be all right?*

"Things are crazy around here," Dove says as we watch the horse. He moves like a dark river flowing through the deep green grass. "Jack and Diana were arguing when I arrived. Colin says he wants to run away."

"He can't run away," I say. Sultan has stopped at a bare spot in the grass. He drops to his knees, like he's bowing to the sun, and then he rolls, his long and beautiful black legs playing with the sky. "Colin's got so much right here," I say. "He's got Diana. He's got Cloudy and Sultan."

He's got me.

to," Diana says. "Let your hands hang by your sides. I'll take control for now. I want you to focus on feeling your horse—how she moves." She walks to the center of the ring and, holding the lunge line with one hand, flicks the whip with her other. "Walk on, Tess."

Tess must have been lunged before. She knows what to do. She moves right out. Ears forward, head held high, she prances around Diana. It feels strange—giving up control. It makes me feel off balance.

"Heels down, Willo. Sit tall," Diana says.

I settle my weight into my heels. Tess and I jog around Diana, who, rope in hand, turns with us. At first, I feel uncomfortable with no reins to cling to; I bounce. But since I don't have to worry about holding Tess back, I concentrate on feeling her. Slowly, gradually, I begin to feel something I haven't felt before—her rhythm. It's an easy beat: one, two, three, four—one, two, three, four. A faint wind fans the back of my neck. *Relax.*

"Now you're getting it. Trot, Tess." Diana flicks the whip. "Trot on."

Tess moves out so briskly I grab her mane and stand in my stirrups. This is scary. This kind of riding is hard!

"Let go of her mane," Diana calls.

I take a deep breath and then let go. I feel awkward as I try to post—rising and falling in the saddle to the

I watched Diana walk uphill to her white-pillared house. I didn't like the way that huge house towered over her; it made her look small.

Three days later, at my ring for Friday's lesson, Diana climbs out of her red Fiat and she smiles over at me. She seems more relaxed now. Maybe she got things ironed out with Jack. She reaches into her car and brings out lunging equipment. Does she mean to lunge Tess and me? Is this her new tactic? Have me ride in circles around her like a beginner while she controls Tess with a long rope and whip?

"Hi Willo." Diana looks up at me, mounted on a horse I've owned for almost two months. I've had more than two years of riding lessons! She says, "We're going to try lunging today. I believe that it will help you two."

I can't answer. I feel as if she's demoting me from eighth grade to kindergarten. Diana doesn't say anything more but I sense her thoughts: *This is something we have to do.*

All right. I square my shoulders. Diana nods. She places a heavy-looking halter over Tess's bridle and then attaches the lunge line to it. She ties the reins high up on Tess's neck. As she leads my mare over to the rail, I feel my face turn red. If Tess and I have to be led everywhere, we'll never make Dad's deadline.

"Don't grab the reins unless you absolutely have

"I can't help it. Oh, I can't keep this a secret any-more, Willo. I just can't," she sobs. "It's not fair to tell me something I can't share with my best friend."

"What is it, Dove?" Is this the secret she hinted at during the pony club meeting last month? And at Josefa's house?

"You can't tell anyone. If Jack finds out—"

"I won't tell." Why do I feel so cold?

"After next week's clinic," she sobs, "there'll be no more Sultan. No Colin. No Diana. They're leaving Jack. They're moving away to Massachusetts. Oh Willo, what will we do without them? This is all so sad."

At midnight I am in the bathroom and throwing up everything I ate at Granddad's and my celebratory dinner. I am possessed by some awful demon who does cartwheels in my stomach. Even after my poor stomach's empty, it goes on vomiting. I am thirsty, but I throw up everything I drink. Finally, Granddad says, "No more water. It just makes things worse."

He thinks it's the curry that's caused all this. But when I wake up the next morning with a sore throat and a fever, we know that curry's not the problem. Something more is going on. I think I've got a broken heart. People die from broken hearts.

On Monday, I'm so sick Granddad insists I see a doctor. I don't want to go. I don't care if I stay sick forever. Maybe I'll die. The doctor says I have the flu. I'll probably be out of school a week. Josefa comes to take care of me. She fixes me soup, puts cool washcloths on my hot forehead and tells me that Celeste hasn't had her kittens yet. Josefa says, "We're afraid our little cat is going to explode."

I know just how she is feeling.

Gram calls the fourth day I'm in bed. "Eat carrots," she tells me. "Eat red Jell-O. Have your grandfather fix you warm milk with celery salt. And Willojean, stay away from carbohydrates after seven P.M. They'll give you gas."

Granddad calls Diana. He cancels what probably would have been my last lesson with her. "You and Tess are very special to Diana," Granddad tells me later. "When I told her of your recent triumph, she said she knew that you had it in you to be partners."

"Diana said that?" I don't think Diana has ever said that about Tess and me.

"She did. She's looking forward to showing you two off to this Ted Walliker. She says he'll teach you some of the finer points of jumping."

"Tess misses you," Dove says on Saturday after I've been sick a week. "I put her and Toby out in the field behind the barn and she went crazy. She galloped all over, looking for you.

"Colin called. He's wondering how we're going to

get our horses to the clinic. He says riding along the highway's no good. We should take the path through the Confederates' Swamp. But there's vines. He'll try to get back there tomorrow. He'll try to clean them out.

"Willo. You have to get better. I'm spending the night with you, remember? We'll have fun. You'll get to see Colin again."

I don't know if I want to see Colin. He didn't tell me he was leaving. Didn't he trust me? I can keep a secret. I never told anyone that he kissed me.

That night, my fever breaks. By Monday, my throat and stomach feel better. I eat chicken noodle soup and toast and I take vitamins to make myself get better fast. I've got to go to the clinic. Not only for Tess and me, but for Colin. You can't leave someone you've kissed without telling them good-bye. You have to say good-bye!

Tuesday, Granddad takes me out to see Tess. She's so glad to see me. She flattens her ears. *Where have you been?* When she kisses me, she almost knocks me down.

I return to school on Wednesday, October 31—a wet and rainy Halloween. Leaves plaster streets and sidewalks. Soggy ghosts hang from lampposts. Plastic skeletons drip water. No trick-or-treating tonight. It's so wet and rainy I don't even let Tess and Toby out to run.

Thursday, November 1, dawns cool and breezy. By late afternoon, the weather turns hot. Strange weather for November. I get off the bus alone because Dove, who often gets off with me, is at an after-school meeting of the art club.

Granddad's at a poker party and I don't feel like entering an empty house. I cut across the front field to the barn. I'll spend time with Tess. I've missed her. And I need to school her for the clinic.

Tess hasn't been ridden in almost two weeks. She's so full of herself. She fights me as we cut across the front field to the sheep's pasture. She wants to gallop. I want her to walk. I grit my teeth, grip the reins and hold her to a high-stepping trot.

Near Crazy's Pond, she shies at a wet leaf and bolts. Four months ago, I would have panicked. Now, settling my weight, I turn her. I canter Tess in ever-tightening circles until I get her stopped.

But I've been sick so long, just riding Tess this little bit has worn me out. And I'm so hot! There's no school tomorrow because the teachers have a conference. I can school Tess in the morning when the weather's cool and fresh. I turn Tess back to the barn. Daylight saving time has ended; it's already growing dark.

The hot day turns into an even hotter, muggy evening. I sweat as I trudge uphill to the house carrying a backpack full of books. The house looks different. It's the lights. Granddad must be home and he's turned on all the lights. Lights downstairs. Lights upstairs. Lights are on in my dad's bedroom. *That's odd.*

I come through the kitchen door as Granddad's taking a tray of ice cubes out of the refrigerator. He gives me a stern look. He hardly ever gives me stern looks.

"What's wrong?" I try to stay calm, but inside, my heart begins to pound.

"The C.O. came home earlier than planned," Granddad says. "He's in the living room. There's something he wants to discuss with you. I suggest you get in there and you talk to him. Now."

CHAPTER 23

Dad sits in the red plaid chair that stands kitty-corner between the living room window and the fireplace. The tan suit he has on is wrinkled from a plane ride. He looks more tired than he did when I saw him four months ago. He'd been all keyed up then, driving us home from Gram's. I hope he's not keyed up now.

"Hi Dad. You're home early," I say, and he says, "I am. And don't I get a hug?"

"Yessir." I hug him and he gives me a "sandpaper kiss"; he rubs his prickly unshaved cheek against my smooth one. He says, "How's eighth grade?"

"Fine." I take a deep breath. "How's work?" Even

before he says, "Not so fine," I know the answer from the bleary defeated look that comes over his eyes. So this is why Granddad looked so stern in the kitchen. This is what Dad and I need to discuss.

"The other week you said you'd made the deadline—"

"I had. My team had. But the U.S. Navy doesn't seem to care about that. What it cares about is money. It's decided, at the last moment, that it can't support my project."

"You mean it's over?"

"The project's dead. God, it's hot in here." Dad parts the living room curtains, opens the window, and I see the moon's reflection. It's shimmering in the creek. The moon is pale and white and almost full. Wind, blowing off the creek, makes the shrouds on the *Bonnie Prince Charlie* go *clinkety-clink*.

"I haven't sailed that boat since last November." Dad sits down. He looks me over. "You've been riding."

"Yessir." Wind, coming through the window, fans the top of Dad's brown hair. From the kitchen comes the clicking sound of ice being poured into a glass. My stomach twists.

"How's the horse?" Dad says.

"She's doing pretty well."

"What do you mean—*pretty* well?" Dad, the engineer, likes things precise. All right.

"She's fattened up. Her scars have healed. I can walk and trot and canter her. The other day, she came on the bit for me."

"I see." He doesn't ask what "on the bit" means. He gives me a funny look. "So. You can control her?" The way he looks at me—like he's testing me or something—warns me, *Be precise, Willo.*

"Yessir. I can."

He gives me that funny look again.

I take a deep breath. "She's doing so well I've been invited to ride her in a special clinic this Saturday."

"This Saturday?"

"Yessir. A jumping clinic. At Diana's. She's bringing in a famous man to teach it. She's only invited the best and most important riders." I know this is a lie, but with Dad, I need one.

As I am saying it, the living room windows come alive with wind. They billow like crazy around Dad. Granddad enters the room. He sees the curtains and says, "Looks like we're in for a storm." He gives Dad a glass of scotch, which he downs in a single gulp. Dad nods to Granddad and then goes on to say, "I could use another."

That night we eat by candlelight. The dining room windows behind Dad reflect the candles' glow. Beyond that, somewhere, is the moon. I long to be outside, sitting on the creek bank, being with that moon. I want to be anywhere but here. Dad is on his fifth drink now.

He's changed into his plaid bathrobe. Light brown chest hair curls out from where he's forgotten to button his pajama top. "So, Willojean's been invited to ride in a jumping clinic." Dad speaks each word precisely.

Granddad says nothing. He hasn't spoken much since I got back from the barn—except to give orders: Wash your hands before supper. Set the table. I say, "That's right, Dad. I've been working Tess hard to get her ready."

"Really? Well, I've been working hard, too. I decided rather than stay in California and stew over a contract gone sour, I'd come home to relax. I'd work on the *Bonnie Prince Charlie.* Go sailing Saturday and Sunday. I figured you could crew for me."

But Mom was the one who always crewed for Dad. She was the one who was good at sailing.

"There's the clinic," I say. "Besides, I'm terrible at sailing, Dad. You know that. The boom always knocks me in the head. Ropes get all tangled around my feet."

"Sailing's not the only thing that seems to give you problems." Dad narrows his eyes. *Here it comes.* I grip my fork so tightly the edge cuts into my fingers. "You think that I don't know what's going on? Only a few hours home from California and I can see. I have eyes.

My walking stick has eyes. It tells me you've been dis-obeying orders, Willo. You've been riding Tess *outside the ring.*"

"But of course I have." I need to make this sound as natural as breathing. Everyone rides their horse out-side the ring. I glance at Granddad. He looks away; he won't look at me. I lied to him—I told him Dad said I could ride Tess where I pleased.

"My orders were explicit," Dad says. "You were not to ride the horse anywhere but in the ring. This after-noon, I took a short walk. I saw you disobeying them. Not only that. I saw Tess run away with you. Again."

He'd been near the front field. Somehow he'd been near the front field. Had seen Tess shy and bolt with me. "No, Dad! She didn't run away. I circled her! I got her stopped! She's not normally so keyed up. It was the first time she'd been ridden in almost two weeks. I've been sick."

"For all I know, she's run away with you a dozen times," he says.

"It was only one time, Roger," Granddad says. "That was before we built the ring."

"It wouldn't matter if Tess ran away with me a thousand times," I say. "All Dad cares about is scotch." I don't believe what I've just said. I'm crazy to have said it.

"Enough of that!" Dad's eyes glitter the way the ice

does in his glass. On his plate, the shepherd's pie Grand-dad fixed sits uneaten—a wedge of mashed potatoes, peas and hamburger, growing cold.

"How were you planning to get Tess to the clinic?" Dad asks.

"Ride her."

"Along Ferry Highway?"

"No, sir. It's too dangerous. There's a shortcut. A back way. Through the woods."

"I see. I've been gone all summer. I've been working day and night and here you two are." He's including Granddad in this. But it's not Granddad's fault. I lied. *I'm sorry, Granddad.* "Plotting behind my back. Disobeying orders. YOU ARE NOT TO RIDE THE HORSE OUTSIDE THE RING!"

"But Dad!"

Granddad looks at me. *Don't say anything more.*

Dad takes a sip of scotch. He takes another. He says, "We had an agreement, Willo. If you couldn't control the horse by November second, you'd get rid of it."

"Her name is Tess. And I can control her."

"I don't think so. For four months, you've been wasting your time on a skinny, scarred, beat-up loser. Tell me, Willo, why do you bother with the horse?" Dad's hand, holding the glass, is shaking. His eyes suddenly look tired. "Give me one good reason."

"Because I love her."

CHAPTER
24

It's hot in my room. Everything is dark except for moonlight coming through the window. I've been crying. The pillow beneath my cheek is damp. From the room below me comes the sad wailing of bagpipes. Dad's listening to one of his Scottish music CDs. The eerie music wails through the house and makes my insides ache.

I throw off my sheets and open the window. A big orange moon—a harvest moon—hangs low in the sky. It lights up the barn where the horse I love is sleeping.

Far to my left, Maiden Creek reflects the moon. I'd like to dive down deep into the moon's reflection.

Swim through moonlit water, and when I came up, why, there would be Dove. She'd crown me with seaweed. Queen Willojean. Colin could be my king. We'd have a palace by the sea. I'd have Tess. He'd have Sultan.

A breeze comes through the window and fans my face. If only Mom could be here. She could talk to Dad for me. I turn so that the breeze can reach my back, and that's when I hear it—a sudden bang. It seems to come from the far side of the creek. There's nothing over there but the broken-down cottage and it's empty. Beyond it, through the short stretch of woods and across Ferry Highway, is Colin and Diana's farm.

There's a second bang. A third. I listen for a fourth. Nothing comes but the drone of bagpipes and the wind through trees. I tell myself those bangs were made by a backfiring truck. Trucks travel this time of night. Don't they? A huge cloud drifts across the moon, and then, the droning of Dad's bagpipe music ceases.

I climb into bed and hug my pillow. I rock and rock until I finally rock myself to sleep. Sleeping, I dream I'm in the house where I used to live with Mom and Dad in California. I'm in the kitchen and my dad is swinging me. My face is pressed against his rough wool sweater. It smells salty, from the sea. He sings, "Willojean. Willojean. Prettiest gal I've ever seen." The kitchen is a happy blur of white cabinets and Blue, our old collie dog, barking at my flying feet.

I am eight years old and Dad has just changed my name from Jillian to Willojean. It's because I'm thin as a willow and always in jeans. He thinks it's just for fun—this nickname he's given me. But I grab it. I make it my own. Because *Willojean* is more me than *Jillian* can ever be.

And this part of the dream is true. In real life, this happened. Dad had come in from sailing. I'd come home from horseback riding. Mom was cooking marzetti for supper and Dad whirled me round. He gave me a name. I loved that name.

But in the dream, there is no Mom and Dad won't stop his swinging. I grow older and taller and skinnier and I yell at him to stop. I have to go to the barn and saddle Tess. I need to get to Colin and Diana. I want Tess and me to go wherever they are going. The more I yell, the faster Dad swings me. He smells funny now. He smells of scotch and he won't let me go. When I reach thirteen, my legs are too long. The kitchen's too small. My feet bang against the cabinets.

Bang. Bang. Bang.

The next morning, my room is cold. It's crazy weather—one moment hot, the next so cold. The clinic starts tonight. I huddle in bed. Tess and I have come so far. I can't give up the clinic. I won't give up Tess. But what to do? It's not until I'm out of bed and in the bathroom brushing my teeth that it comes to me. Tess and I will go to Diana's, like I wanted to in my dream. We'll go today and hide out there for the night. I bet Colin would help us do that. After tomorrow's lesson with Ted Walliker, I'll call Dad and maybe Diana will speak to him for me. She'll say, "Willojean and Tess belong together." If Dad says, "No they don't," I'll stay at Diana's. I'll go with her and Colin to Massachusetts and never come home—ever!

I throw on a T-shirt, jeans and my beautiful black boots. I grab a jacket and an extra pair of underpants and socks. I run downstairs, and as I do most mornings, I grab the banister to jump across the landing outside Granddad's office. Will I clear it today? The heels of my feet catch on the steps and I fall backward, knocking my head. As usual. No one calls out, "Willojean? Are you all right?"

Dad and Granddad are gone. They've drunk coffee. I can tell by the empty pot. Two mugs. A newspaper on the kitchen table has been left open to the weather page. Rising, then plunging temperatures are predicted along with high winds. Dad loves high winds. He did want to go sailing today. That's where he must be now—sailing. Granddad's note says, *Running errands. Be back around noon.*

Good.

I walk downhill to the barn with a strong wind at my back. I imagine Dad hoisting the spinnaker to catch it. The wind will fill the gaily striped sail and propel Dad's boat so fast it will feel like a plane accelerating for takeoff. It will take Dad out of Maiden Creek and into Wyndham River. He'll be gone for hours.

CHAPTER 25

Leaves swirl through the barn's open doorway. Leaves spin crazily across the floor in front of Tess's hooves. I've tethered her to crossties. While I groom her, she stares at cloud shadows racing across the barnyard, darkening the oak tree, the manure pile and, now, the wooden gate.

I work my curry comb toward dried mud on Tess's belly and her ears go back. She lifts a hind leg, warning me to stop. Four months ago, I would have. Now, I croon gently and break up the mud as gently as I can.

"Willo!" It's Dove. I didn't think she'd be here so early. She fumbles with the gate. It groans, then swings wide open. She races across the barnyard. Her gray flannel shirt billows out like wings. Her curly hair seems alive with wind. She runs at me, gasping, "Willo. You won't believe it!"

Tess dances backward. She yanks furiously against the crossties that confine her. Before she can break her halter like she did so long ago, I grab it and unsnap the ropes. Hooves scrambling on the concrete floor, she drags me down the hall until her hindquarters smash against her stall door. *Bang.*

"You silly horse. It's Dove. It's only Dove." I try to keep my voice calm, but inside I'm shaking.

Dove approaches more slowly now. She offers Tess a sugar cube.

"You can't run up on her like that!"

"I'm sorry." Dove watches Tess gobble up the treat and then offers her another. "It's just . . . last night, Celeste had her kittens, Willo. Five of them. On my bed.

"I was there. I watched her push four calico kittens out, one after the other. And then, the fifth one's head got stuck." A sudden quiet comes over Dove.

"Don't tell me something awful happened." I can't take any more awful stuff. I rest my cheek against Tess's neck. Calmer now, she nuzzles my stomach.

"The kitten's head was about halfway out," Dove says. "This sweet, dark-furred head. It was too big for Celeste to push. I got one of Mom's rags—a rough piece of an old washcloth—to give me a good grip." Dove holds up her hands. "I worked my thumb and index finger around the kitten's head. I was so scared— afraid I'd hurt Celeste."

"You should have called the vet."

"There wasn't time. And no one was home. I read about how to do this in my cat book. Celeste knew I wanted to help. As she pushed, I pulled. The kitten didn't budge. Celeste pushed. I pulled.

"I was all upset and crying. Afraid she'd die. The kitten was too big. Celeste, too small. It was hopeless. It would never work. Just as I was about to give up, Celeste eee-oowwed. She pushed. I pulled and the kitten popped out. This wet dark ball of fur slipped into my hand just as easy as you please. It was like a miracle.

"Now there's not only Celeste to cuddle, but five kittens as well. Four calicos and the dark one. His color's like Sultan's—the color of your creek at night. He's so cute." Dove brings Toby out and hitches him to crossties. "Hey, am I still spending tonight with you?"

"Tonight?" Tess drags me to Toby. She blows softly into his unruly mane.

"Tonight, Willo. The clinic starts tonight."

"Oh yeah." So much has been going on, I forgot about Dove's staying with me. Should I tell her she can't? That I'm hiding out at Diana's? No. Not until we get there.

"I may be late for the clinic." Dove looks funny, as if I'm supposed to know why. "Today's November second, Willo. All Souls' Day. The Day of the Dead." She's just delivered kittens and now she's talking about the dead? She's as topsy-turvy as the weather—cold, then hot, and now so windy. "I have to go to the cemetery with Grandma Josefa," she says. "The way that you and I did last year. Remember?"

I remember. Mom had just come home from the hospital. There'd been wind and leaves just like today. In the cemetery, I'd carried a plate of tamales, while beside me, Dove carried candles. Josefa, arms filled with yellow and orange marigolds, led us through a maze of tombstones toward her husband's grave. "America is a sad place," she told us. "No one honors the dead the way we do in Mexico. The souls of the dead return to visit for one day out of all the year and none of your families come out to greet them. No one offers them food to eat. They are all forgotten. When I am gone, I will be forgotten, too."

"No, you won't!" Dove and I both told her.

She turned and smiled—large and warm and real in the chilly twilight. She stopped before a large gray tombstone. "Here he is."

Josefa arranged flowers around the plate of food that she set on her husband's grave. She brought out a necklace of black beads. She fingered one bead after another, while she prayed in Spanish for him. Then she lit candles. She said the flames were needed to guide her husband's visiting soul back to its grave and from there to heaven. I shivered as I watched the flames, for I wondered where, in the gathering dark, her husband's soul might be.

Yes. I remember last year's November 2. I won't forget this year's either. From the barn, I can see clouds boiling through the sky. The wind smells of rotting apples and autumn leaves. I wish I could visit my mom's grave. I'd light candles. I'd say prayers. I'd tell her about the miracle of Celeste and her five kittens. I'd tell her about Tess and my going to Diana's. I need my mom. Oh, why did she have to die?

CHAPTER
26

I think the souls of the dead come back as leaves; today there are so many of them. Alive with wind, they crackle across the manure pile and get caught up in the barnyard fence. Tess, bridled head held high, watches as a burst of leaves colors the sky above the nearby Christmas trees.

Dove leads Toby outside and buckles her hard hat. "To the ring!"

"Not today. I want to try out the trail Colin cleared through the Confederates' Swamp. I want to see him and Diana." Before Dove can question this, I swing up on Tess. I'm not even in the saddle and she trots off through the open gate. I grab her mane to steady myself and, with my right foot, search for the stirrup.

Still in the barnyard, Dove calls, "Wait for me!"

Tess extends her trot. I find the stirrup, then abandon her mane to grab the reins. I close my hands on them. She throws her head, fighting me. The wind tears at my face. For a moment, we struggle. For a moment, I panic: *Can I control this horse?* I think of a rope anchored to something so deep inside me nothing can dislodge it. I grab hold. I settle in the saddle and tighten my reins. I feel Tess giving in. "Good girl." I open my hands slightly. Her reward.

She settles her power beneath me. *See that, Dad?* Beneath Tess's hooves, gravel flies. Scrub trees, littering the front field, rustle with wind. Canadian geese, startled by her, lift off Crazy's Pond. They honk wildly— *Go back.*

Tess leans on the bit, asking to canter. Now that I'm in control, a part of me wants to let her go. Wants her to gallop so fast I can't feel her moving beneath me. We'll gallop together to the ends of the earth, and then, we'll plunge into deep and wonderful piles of leaves.

"Hey Willo! Wait!" Dove calls.

I slow Tess so that Dove and Toby can catch up. We trot together through the gate and into the wild field with the silo. A path the horses have made winds through deep grass Granddad hasn't had time to cut. A shadow crosses this path. The silo's shadow.

Today, the ugly tan silo, crumbling from where lightning struck it, is full of moaning wind—*Go back.* Should I? No. I've never ridden to Diana's and now's the time. As Tess trots through the silo's long dark shadow, I feel my skin grow cold.

At the far end of the field, Tess and I follow Dove through a break in the barbed-wire fence where deerflies once attacked me. There are no deerflies today. Just the restless wind and leaves. Our horses take a path I've never been down. My stomach turns queasy. *There's quicksand back here.*

The path angles down a steep and rocky hill. Shadows cast by branches make a jigsaw puzzle out of everything—the path, Dove and Toby, the thick dense brush. Above us, swaying vines link one tree to another. Tess, nose pressed anxiously against Toby's tail, jerks at the bit. She slathers spit on Toby's rump. His tail swishes a mild warning: *Keep back.*

"Easy, Tess."

The path skirts a vine-choked well—a half-circle of crumbling brick that's built into the slope. A spring bubbles out from it. Is this where the Confederate soldiers camped?

The path dips sharply and Tess's forequarters drop

out from under me. I lean back in the saddle and she half slides, half trots down the slope, her hooves scattering chunks of faded brick. Vines that Colin uprooted lie scattered along the path. Sweat breaks out along Tess's neck. She follows Toby toward the bottomland and swamp.

Brown leaves float on pools of stagnant water. Limbless trees rise out of the marsh. It smells like Maiden Creek back here—a mix of brackish water, rotting reeds and mud.

"The fork where we veer off to Diana's can't be far," I call to Dove. Something plops into water off to my left. "What was that?"

"A frog," she says.

"There aren't any frogs in November."

Tess mouths her bit. Mud sucks at her hooves. Patches of swamp, thick undergrowth and trees crowd her on either side. Ahead, the path forks. The right branch swerves east and downhill, following the swampy trickle of a stream through deepening woods of tall green hemlocks. The left fork curls uphill through sunlight. This must be the path to Diana's. A skinny log propped between two trees crosses it. Did Colin set up a jump for us? It's only about two feet high.

"I'll take the jump first," Dove calls. "Then Tess can follow. Hold her back until Toby clears it. Okay?" Dove kicks her pony into a canter before I have the chance to say it's not okay. That Tess goes crazy if she's left behind. Dove knows this. Dove's not thinking.

Tess lunges at the bit, but I hold firm; I don't let her have it. I keep my heels away from her sides. I sense that all she needs is one excuse, a little pressure in the wrong place, and she'll explode. She dances impatiently from one foreleg to the other. She whinnies to Toby. *Don't leave.*

Toby canters toward the jump. Dove rises in her stirrups. She perches like a small bird over Toby's back. He gathers himself, and Tess, since she can't move forward, starts dancing sideways. "Tess! Knock it off!"

She rams her rump against a tree. As she edges backward around it, I throw my left leg over her shoulder so that I won't get squished. Vines grab at my hard hat. A tree branch whips against my face. Her hindquarters slip off the path and into swampy undergrowth. Her hooves flounder backward through mud. With my legs, I urge Tess to go forward. She backs up.

Her hindquarters start to sink beneath me. *There's quicksand here. If we get caught in quicksand, we're goners.* I loosen the reins. Keeping low to Tess's neck, I do something I wouldn't ordinarily do. I kick her hard. The stubborn horse. She doesn't move. Her hooves don't move.

"Tess!" I slam my heels into her sides. She grows still. I feel her gathering beneath me. I slam again and she explodes—plunging forward, ripping through briars and vines. She bucks. She kicks to free herself. I lose both stirrups. She pulls the reins out of my hands.

She scrambles back onto the path. She gallops toward Dove and Toby, who wait for us uphill from the jump they've taken. I don't want to take the jump now.

"Whoa, Tess." I grab the reins and pull. She won't listen. She barrels toward the jump that separates her from Toby. Up close, the jump looks big and hard and scary. Tess, ears flattened, lifts beneath me. She soars as if the jump were six feet high instead of two. When she lands, she throws me off balance.

Half on, half off, I cling to her neck. She plunges uphill. Now that she's running, she doesn't want to stop. She passes a startled Dove. She passes a huge downed tree. She gallops faster, faster still. My heart pounds in my throat. Her thundering hooves become my heartbeats. "Stop, Tess. Stop!"

Dove cries, "Willojean!"

The path, bordered by thick firs, levels off. Ahead is a steep bank falling to the creek. I imagine Tess and me plummeting through sky, crashing into mud and water. I try to right myself. Tess's shoulder moves against my chest. My right leg, still draped across her haunches, slips. Someone steps out from the fir trees.

I see a red plaid shirt. A walking stick. Dad? I thought he was—

Tess shies from him and I am falling. The ground slams into me. I hold on to Tess's reins. I'm not about to let her go. She drags me over bruising stones and roots. Just as I fear she'll never stop, she does. Near the edge of the steep bank—brown reeds, dark mud and shimmering water spreading out below.

I scramble to my feet. Dad's approaching. I feel his burning gaze. Four months of anger come boiling out of me.

"You stupid horse." I jerk Tess's reins. I slam the bit against her teeth. Eyes rolling, looking hurt, she backs away. Still holding on to her, I grab a stick. Sobbing, I whip the stick back and forth across her neck and chest. "Go on. Back yourself into the creek," I sob. "Drown yourself. What do I care?"

CHAPTER 27

Tess's stall is warm and dark. I've folded myself into her manger and she munches on hay caught between my knees. I try not to look at the welts I made on her neck and chest, but they're at eye level. It makes me hurt to see the raised and swollen skin.

In the woods, Dad put his hand on my arm and said, "Stop beating her, Willo." I paused. Dad's eyes met mine. There was not the anger I expected; there was sadness. I looked away. I saw a panicked Tess and thought, *Oh my God, what have I done?*

She took up all my attention then. Tess was wild with hurt. She felt betrayed. I was no better than all the others who'd abused her. *Hang me from the yardarms. Let seagulls pick my flesh.* Dad's voice, at my back, grew stern. "Don't mount her again. Walk her to the barn.

"We'll talk about this later."

I never heard him leave. But by the time Dove had ridden up on Toby, he was gone. I'm afraid to see him later. Afraid to talk to him. How can I explain why I was in the swamp? How can I tell him—"I was going to Diana's and maybe leave you forever. It's so hard to talk to you"?

Tess regards me with dark eyes that are gentle-looking now. "Oh, Tess. I'm sorry." I reach out. I place my hand on a welt I made. Tess doesn't flinch. She doesn't move away. "Why'd you go and act so crazy?"

I rest my head and shoulder against the worn, smooth manger slats. It's one o'clock in the afternoon, but it feels like dusk. It's all dark in here and cozy. Tess and Toby make the only sounds, chomping hay. Dove left the barn over two hours ago. She apologized for taking off on Toby. "I'm sorry, Willo. I didn't think. I'll learn to think. I promise!

"When did your dad come home? You never told me he'd come home."

With my finger, I trace the deep hollows over Tess's eyes, the white swirl of hair caught in the middle of her star. She shifts her weight, rustling the thick straw cushioning her hooves. I run my hand down her crooked stripe to her muzzle. She nuzzles me, then rests her nose in the hollow between my chest and knees.

I wrap my arms around her head and cry. Tess doesn't panic, as I fear she might. She blows softly, in and out. In and out. I love this horse; she is so forgiving. She lets me cradle her the way her manger cradles me.

It's midafternoon and hot. Over 80 degrees and hazy. Outside the barn, the wind has died. My skin's clammy with the heat. The Christmas trees near the barnyard look hot and dry, the way they did in summer. Today's paper said it's supposed to rain. Sometime tonight or tomorrow we'll have rain.

Granddad's car isn't in the garage, but Dad's is. I come through the kitchen door and there he is with sleeves rolled up, standing at the sink. Suds cover his arms up to the elbows. Dad washing dishes is as strange as the weather. He never washes dishes.

Boswell sits on the kitchen table, where he knows he's not allowed. His head turns; his green eyes fasten on me. He looks angry. I broke the rules. I hurt a fellow animal, Tess, his friend and rival.

Without turning round, Dad says, "You missed

lunch." This is not a Dad kind of thing to say. He never worries about me and lunch. That's Granddad's territory. Has everything gone topsy-turvy?

"I wasn't hungry." I pick up Boswell. He lets me cuddle him—his purrs warming my chest. Bozzie forgives me. "Where's Granddad?"

"Still running errands, I imagine. Are you okay?"

"I guess so."

"And what about Tess?" He's asking about the horse that last night he called a beat-up loser? My throat tightens. Tears blur my eyes. "She's not okay. She may never be okay. What I did to her today was a big mistake and I am going to regret it from now into eternity."

"We all make mistakes," Dad says, "a fact which became all too apparent to me in the woods today."

I stare at Dad. "What do you mean?"

"I drink too much." He admits it just like that. He never admits this kind of thing. Oh, this is a strange day. A wild day. He says, "When I drink, I come down too hard on you. I'm sorry, Willo." Dad clears his throat. "There's something more I have to tell you."

"What?" The something's bad. I can tell by Dad's tone, it's really bad. "Did something happen to Granddad? You told me Granddad was at the store!" I can't keep the panic out of my voice.

"No. He's fine." Dad's eyes search mine.

"What is it?"

"Sultan," he says. Dad's never met the horse. What does he know about Sultan? Or Diana. Or Colin. Anything that means everything to me. "Dove called a few minutes ago," Dad says. "She told me to tell you that last night—" Dad pauses. He takes a deep breath and lets it out. "Last night, Sultan attacked Jack, and so, Jack had to shoot him."

"No." I grip Bozzie so tightly he jumps out of my arms. He lands on a pan Dad set on the table—*bang*. The sound reminds me of last night. *Bang. Bang. Bang.* "I don't believe it!"

"I wish you didn't have to." Dad says this as if he really means it. How can he mean it? He doesn't know how I feel about Sultan—so wild and powerful. When he moved, he flowed like a river.

"Colin loved Sultan. Diana loved him. You don't get rid of a horse someone loves. Ever! It's their choice whether to keep the horse. Not yours."

"I know." Dad holds out his sudsy hands. He wants me to run into his arms? Let him comfort me after all that's happened? All the months he's been away? All the months of drinking? He hates Tess. He called my horse a loser. He's no better than Jack!

"Come here, Willo," Dad says softly.

"No. No!" I back away. "This is all a lie. A horrible, terrible lie."

CHAPTER
28

At dinner, Dad carries a glass of red wine into the dining room to drink with the vegetable and beef soup Granddad's prepared. To cheer things up and make the world seem nicer, Granddad made me put a white cloth and a vase of yellow chrysanthemums on the table where Dad's setting his drink right now. I didn't want to pick the flowers. Mom planted those chrysanthemums a year ago this August and now she's gone and so is Sultan.

Dove had called and confirmed what Dad had already told me. "Jack shot him last night," she said. "Three times, Willo."

I heard those shots.

"This morning, Colin had to help bury Sultan in the front field. Colin's a mess. He could barely talk to me. Jack left for a business conference in Florida. When he comes back, Colin and Diana will be gone.

"Diana's still holding the clinic," Dove said.

"How can she?"

"She's doing it for us. She wants us to meet Ted Walliker. He could be our new riding instructor, Willo. He's looking for students."

I'm not looking for a teacher.

The crystal chandelier above the table is reflecting candlelight. Stars of light dance across Dad's folded hands; he's about to pray. He bows his head, so I bow mine. He says:

God grant us the courage to change those things we can,
The serenity to accept those things we can't,
And the wisdom to know the difference.

I know this prayer. Dad often says it when he's on the wagon, which means he's not drinking. He's not on the wagon now. The wine decanter on the table next to his place mat is almost empty. Did he empty it because of me?

I'm too upset to eat. I fiddle with my soup. If I can make the corn, which I love, float on one side and the peas, which I hate, float on the other, then Dad will

185

stop drinking. Jack will stay forever in Florida. Diana and Colin won't move away. Life will go on and Tess will—

"Willojean?" Dad says the first word to me since I'd run out of the kitchen.

"Yessir." A carrot piece pops up on the pea side. I put it with the corn.

"Your grandfather's been telling me about you and Tess." *He has?* I glance at Granddad. He's said nothing to me about what went on this morning. He's just had me cut flowers and set the table.

"He tells me you've worked hard," Dad says. "The other day, you got Tess to come on the bit for you. What does this mean—on the bit?"

I feel my throat tighten. Will I ever get Tess on the bit again? "It means your horse trusts you enough to place her weight in your hands." I take a deep breath.

"Tell me more," Dad says.

"She allows all her power to be controlled by these." I hold up my hands. They're shaking. "Once a horse is on the bit, she can take most anything that gets in her way. Like jumps." I put my shaking hands into my lap.

"I see. Go on."

I look across the table at him. Dad's eyes rest on mine. "It's total communication," I say. "You use your seat and legs to generate the power, and then, that power comes forward into your hands. It's magical. Why, it feels like . . ." I try to think of something Dad will understand. "Like sailing the way you did with Mom. That last time. In November."

A pained look crosses Dad's face. I shouldn't have said what I just did. But Mom's gone. Not talking about her won't change that.

"Can you get Tess on the bit again?" Dad says.

"I think so." I've only done it once. But maybe with Diana's help . . . *No. Diana can't help. She's leaving.*

"If you can get her on the bit, I'd say—keep her." Dad tosses down half a glass of wine. From the decanter, he pours what little wine is left.

"You'll show me tomorrow," he says. "Somewhere outside the ring. I need to see that you can ride her in—how shall I put it—the unpredictable places."

"Yessir." I go back to fiddling with my soup. For a moment, I have it—everything lined up. One side, corn with carrots. The other side, peas. *Yes. Everything will work out fine.* And then, Dad gets up to fill the empty wine decanter and jostles the table.

I sit on a fallen log that juts out into the creek. Mudflats stretch out on either side of me. In less than one hour, I am going to Diana's house. Granddad called her to make certain the clinic was still on. Diana said, "Of course. Everyone's looking forward to it. I hope Willo can still come. I want her to meet Ted. He knows how to train jumpers."

I don't want to meet Ted. I love Diana. She's my teacher and she always will be. But I know I need to go for Tess.

A full moon's rising over the creek. The trees along the distant bank look stark—their leafless branches trying to hold back the night. The wind picks up. Uneasy waves lap the shore. It's the Day of the Dead. Dad must be thinking of Mom, because up the hill in back of me, bagpipes from one of their CDs wails a favorite song—the "Skye Boat Song":

> *Speed bonnie boat, like a bird on a wing;*
> *Onward, the sailors cry:*
> *Carry the lad that's born to be king*
> *Over the sea to Skye.*

Dad has told me that Skye's an island off the coast of Scotland. In 1746, Bonnie Prince Charlie fled there after being defeated in the bloody battle of Culloden. From the way the music sounds, Skye must be sad and lonely and full of ghosts. Why would anyone born to be king have to go there?

CHAPTER
29

Four white pillars and a wide front porch, all lit up by spotlights, overlook the field where Sultan once galloped and where he now is buried. Diana's house looks huge and white. I believe every single light is on. Room lights. Porch lights. Outdoor spotlights. Granddad draws in his breath as he turns our car onto the graveled driveway. He says, "I don't care if Sultan did attack Jack. The man had no business shooting him. The horse was Diana's."

Spotlights blaze along the back field. They light up the riding ring where, tomorrow, Ted Walliker will hold classes. In the middle, jumps, including three post and rails, a brush fence and a chicken coop, have already been set up.

In June, I watched Diana gallop Sultan past bright green cornstalks that now have browned and withered. I saw her rise over Sultan's neck. He, in turn, rose beneath her to take a four-foot post and rail. And now, he's gone.

Granddad stops the car at Diana's back door. He stares out the windshield at the darkened sky. A rising wind whips leaves against the car. "While you were at the creek, I talked with our commander," Granddad says. "I told him how proud you'd made me—working hard with Tess. You'll work hard with her again. You're not the type to give up."

"No, sir. I'm not."

Circling his hand, Granddad wipes off steam that's formed on the inside of the car window. "Your father needs tonight to mourn, Willo. Not only the cancellation of his project, but your mother's death. He has trouble saying good-bye."

Me, too.

"He told me that after tonight, there'll be no more drinking," Granddad says.

Dad has said this kind of thing before. Many times. To Mom. "Did he promise?" I say. If Dad promises, it could work this time. Dad never breaks a promise.

"No," Granddad says, and my heart sinks. "But as

your dad and I were talking, your dad pulled a book off the shelf. He paged it open to a favorite poem. When he read the poem aloud to me, it raised the hairs along the back of my neck. The poem was about hope, Willo."

" 'The Darkling Thrush'—'I leant upon a coppice gate when Frost was spectre-gray . . . ' I know the poem by heart. It took me a while to memorize it—the words are complicated and hard. But I love that poem."

"It's a fine poem. Now and again, say it to yourself. Now you go on. Give that fine woman Diana a hug for me." Granddad pats my shoulder. He smooths down my hair. As soon as I step out of the car, a gust of wind catches my hair and blows it all over my face. The wind sends leaves scuttling across the seven concrete squares that lead from Granddad's car to the house.

I knock at the door and Diana answers. She's talking to someone over her shoulder, so she doesn't see me at first. She looks different. It's not only her short hair. It's her cheeks. Usually they're olive-colored like the rest of her skin. Tonight, they're red. Her eyes glow so warmly when she sees me. "Willo. I'm so glad you're here."

"Me, too." Tears well in my eyes. "I'm sorry," I say. "It's just a rainy day." I try to smile at Diana through my tears. She touches my cheek. She smooths my hair the way Granddad did. Oh, it's really raining now.

"Laura?" Diana calls over her shoulder to someone in the next room. "Would you man the door for me a minute? I need to talk to someone.

"Let's go someplace private." Diana steers me past a group of kids talking in the hall. Taking my hand, she leads me upstairs to her bedroom. I have always thought it pretty—with its gray carpet, pink-flowered curtains and dressing table with bottles of perfume and a silver-backed brush. Diana sits me down on her bed and she hands me a tissue.

"I've been through a few tissues myself." She sits down beside me. I dab my eyes and blow my nose. I stare at her hands—her beautiful long fingers. I remember red nail polish, the exact color of a bow she'd tied in Sultan's mane. She's not wearing nail polish now. She probably won't ever wear it again. It's raining so hard now I can't see.

"Oh, my dear sweet Willo." Diana puts her arm around me.

"Tonight, at dinner," I sob, "I thought, if I can just make the peas in my soup stay on one side and the corn and carrots stay on the other, everything will turn out all right. I'll be a good rider. Good to Tess. You and Colin will never leave."

"You know we're leaving." She states this as a fact.

"I haven't told anyone. I won't. I promise—"

"I'm glad you know." Diana is holding me the way

a mom would do. Her arm's around me. Her cheek rests against the top of my head and my cheek's pressed against her chest. I can hear her heartbeat.

"I'm moving to Massachusetts, Willo. I'll be with my family—my mother and three brothers. It's all worked out. I'll have a job. I'll board Sweets and Cloudy at the stable where I'll be working. Colin will attend school with his cousins—they've always been good friends.

"We'll be fine and so will you. You have Tess, the farm, your family—your father and that wonderful grandfather of yours."

"I have Gram." With the tissue, I wipe my eyes. "She likes to play bingo and she wears funny hats. I want her to marry Granddad. They belong together."

Diana chuckles. "Oh, Willo. You're so full of love. For people. For animals—"

"I had a little trouble with Tess today."

"Your grandfather told me." Diana sighs. I can feel that sigh deep down in my bones. "Tomorrow, you'll get back on her. You'll hold on to that rope we talked about. It's anchored to something so good and deep inside you, nothing can dislodge it. Your love for Tess.

"You are so very special to me." Diana gives me a gentle squeeze. From the floor below us come the sounds of voices. The opening and closing of doors.

For several moments we don't move. I wish I could

stay forever with Diana's arm around me. But then I couldn't ride Tess. Cook curry sauce with Granddad. Eat Gram's jellied cucumbers or help cover Mas-Que Farm with Christmas trees. "Will you be all right?" Diana lifts my chin and looks at me. She has tears in her eyes, too.

I nod. "Can I stay up here a little?" I'm not ready to face regular people just yet.

"Of course you can." As soon as she stands and walks to the door, I miss her warmth. "I'm sorry for what happened to Sultan," I say.

She stops. She turns, her hand on the doorknob. "Me, too."

"Good-bye, Diana." I have to say this now while we are alone and I can deeply mean it. If I don't say good-bye to her, we'll roast in hell. " 'Good-bye' means God be with you."

She smiles softly at me. "God be with you, Willo-jean."

After she's gone, I stretch out on her queen-sized bed. I know her side because the pillow smells like incense—the exotic kind from India, where women have holy circles on their foreheads. Listening to voices coming from below, I hug Diana's pillow. I rock and rock. The bed is soft and warm. It smells of incense and is as comfortable as sleep.

CHAPTER
30

Dad's bagpipe music is still playing when Josefa drops Dove and me off from a program I didn't attend because I slept the whole way through it. Diana made certain I met Ted Walliker, though. He seemed nice, but my attention was all taken up by Colin. His back to me, he gazed out the dining room window, which overlooks the front field. He stood so still at the window. I wanted to close his eyes and put coins on each of his eyelids. According to Granddad, they do that in China to attract good luck and happiness to both the living and the dead.

Dad, dressed in his plaid bathrobe, now marches

slowly across our living room. It's a Scottish funeral march and he's pretending to play a bagpipe. He places one foot precisely in front of the other, as if he's walking a thin, straight line. I am so embarrassed by him. I link my arm through Dove's and take her directly to my room.

"Things aren't going so well around here," I tell Dove as I shut the door. It muffles but it can't drown out the moaning sound of bagpipes. "The Navy canceled Dad's project. He's upset with me. He misses Mom."

"It's okay, Willo. I understand. He's in mourning." Dove knows about mourning. Today she spent two hours at her grandpa's grave. Tonight, the car that Josefa drove us home in smelled of the tamales and marigolds they placed on that grave.

"I didn't get to talk to Colin. How was he?" I say.

"He barely talked to me. It's like he's gone off into some other world. Like he's out there in the darkness with Sultan." Dove opens my window. The color of the windy night beyond reminds me of Sultan and wet leaves.

"We should bring flowers and food to Sultan's grave," Dove says. "We should pray for him, Willo. Tonight. You, me and Colin. If we don't all pray for Sultan, and pray hard, he'll end up in purgatory."

"What's purgatory?" It sounds like hell.

"An awful place you go to right after you die. It's where you suffer for all your sins. You roll gigantic boulders up steep hills. People stick you with burning splinters. They chain you to rocks, and eagles eat out your liver," Dove says. Below us, the droning sound of bagpipes ceases so abruptly it feels as if the house has lost its heartbeat.

"I don't want Sultan to go to purgatory," I say.

"We'll need flowers for his grave."

"I have chrysanthemums."

"And food. Grandma Josefa always puts out food. It helps to feed the spirit." Dove pauses. The wind rattles at the shingles of Granddad's old house. We hear footsteps; Dad and Granddad, coming upstairs to bed.

"We'll bring corn," I whisper. "But we need something more, Dove. Something permanent to mark his grave forever and ever. That way, Sultan will know he's loved, he's been prayed for, he will never be forgotten. Diana will see it and know it, too."

"You want a tombstone," Dove says.

"It doesn't have to be a tombstone."

"Then what?" Dove looks at her watch. "It's already after ten P.M. You'd better think fast. We need to be at the grave before midnight. Midnight marks the end of All Souls Day, the Day of the Dead. Right now, people all over are praying for souls in purgatory. We need to tap into that."

I close my eyes. "Be quiet a moment. Let me think." What could we use to mark a grave? After several moments, I say, "Nothing comes."

"Keep thinking."

I press my palms against my eyes. All I see is darkness. I press a little harder. I see red blobs and then, white lights. Beautiful white lights. This leads me into thinking about Christmas trees.

It's after eleven o'clock. Wispy clouds race across the moonlit sky. I've never seen clouds doing this at night. It seems as if all the wind in the world has retreated into heaven. Down below, everything's so still—like it was in Granddad's house when we snuck downstairs. The only sound now is Dove, spading dirt. It's cold out here in the field beside the barnyard. I pull my jacket close. I clutch the piece of burlap I'm holding and tell Dove, "Hurry up."

"I have to be careful. I don't want to hurt the little roots. There." She throws the spade on the ground. "Now wrap the burlap around them."

She shoulders the little Christmas tree that she's dug up for us to plant on Sultan's grave. I carry the chrysanthemums. Our pockets bulge with corn from the feed bin. We march uphill. Nearing Granddad's house, we grow furtive, sneaking past it and downhill to where *The Admiral* is docked.

The tide is out and the shore is white with shells from an oyster bar that stood here long before Grand-dad's time. Dove crawls into *The Admiral*'s bow. Oyster shells screech as I push the rowboat out, then climb over the stern to the middle seat.

I settle the oars in their locks. Maiden Creek, dark and restless, floats us past Dad's sailboat. It looks like a ghost ship in the moonlight. Its lines hum. The shrouds clink. Clouds soar through the sky overhead. I pull on *The Admiral*'s oars. The oarlocks grumble. *Creak, ka-thump. Creak, ka-thump.*

"Shhhh," Dove hisses.

"I can't 'shhhh.' *The Admiral*'s an old boat. It can't help being noisy." I don't tell Dove this might be the way an old boat protests what we're doing—sneaking out at night. I hope that no one is awake to hear or see us.

"I've never snuck out like this," Dove says. "Not after dark on the Day of the Dead.

"You're heading for the wrong dock, Willo. Pull harder on the left oar," she says, and then, "I guess it's too late to turn back."

"That's right."

"Tell me something to make me feel brave."

"I don't know much about being brave." When I say this, Dove looks so lost I know I have to think of something. After a few moments, I say, "There's this

199

poem I know. It's about a sad man. It's winter and he's outside. The wind moans and the earth feels like a giant grave. Everything's dying. Suddenly, in the middle of it all, this wood thrush—he's really small and frail and old, you wouldn't think he could do anything right—starts singing. He flings his very soul out on the gloom by singing! But why would he sing here and now? In the darkest place? At the darkest hour?"

"I don't know," Dove says.

"He knows that in spite of all the bad things coming down, there's hope for good. And he's going to sing about that hope no matter what." I think of Dad when I say this.

"How's this supposed to make *me* feel brave?" Dove says.

"Think of it this way. It's really dark right now and we're that little thrush. What we're about to do for Sultan will be our song." I surprise myself by saying this. I ship the oars. We've reached shore.

Dove climbs out of *The Admiral* and pulls the bow up onto a mudflat. "Willo, what does it mean to throw your soul out on the gloom?"

"I don't know, Dove. But I sure like the sound of it." I grab the Christmas tree and step out into mud.

"I hope Colin will like the sound of it," she says.

"What do you mean?"

"I've never seen him like he was tonight. It's as if

some silent stranger has taken over his body and the Colin I've always known has died."

All the lights are turned off at Diana's house. The moon has disappeared behind a heavy bank of clouds. Everything is dark. I don't think anyone can see us, but even so, I suck in my stomach and flatten myself against a lamppost. What if Jack missed his plane? What if Jack came back? He owns guns.

From behind a bush, Dove throws a pebble at Colin's window to wake him up. The pebble bounces off the glass, onto the small overhang above the garage, and from there to the ground. She throws a second pebble. A third. *Wake up, Colin.* The pebbles falling make a cantering sound. *Da-da-dump. Da-da-dump.*

The night is silent except for falling pebbles. The night smells of leaves. I shiver against the ice-cold lamppost. Dove throws a fourth pebble. A fifth.

"Shhhh," I hiss. Jack could be home. Jack could hear. He shot Sultan. Three times.

Moments pass. Colin doesn't open the window. Another pebble sings out. Still another. Maybe it's the darkness, the cold, and being scared, but suddenly, it seems to me the noise of the pebbles falling is some sad and lonely spirit calling out. A horse's spirit, calling out, *Please help me.*

"What's going on?" a voice behind me says.

I bite my hand, stifling a scream. *Colin.* He's bare to the waist. He holds a scythe right above the bush where Dove's hiding.

"Don't shoot." She rises slowly, empty hands raised above her head.

"What are you doing here?" He lowers the scythe.

"We need your help," I say. "We want to plant a Christmas tree."

CHAPTER
31

This is stupid. It's not going to make a difference to anyone or anything," Colin says. He stands on Sultan's grave and jabs at dirt with the shovel Dove made him grab from his garage. We made a mistake—throwing stones at Colin's window. We never should have awakened him. The mood he's in, he'll soon be jabbing the shovel at us. I can't believe this is the Colin of my dreams: the Colin who kissed me.

"It will make a difference," Dove says.

"Planting a Christmas tree to mark a horse's grave is stupid," Colin says. "So is all this corn and flowers."

"It's not stupid," I say. A light wind starts to rustle through the cornstalks on the far side of the fence. Cornstalks talk in whispers. They agree with me. I check my watch. It's getting close to midnight. We need to get this over with. Colin steps on the edge of the shovel. He sends its blade deep into the soft dirt a front loader unearthed just yesterday.

"You don't need to dig so deep," Dove says.

"I'm doing this my way." He throws another shovelful of dirt aside. In the moonlight, he looks like Jack. It's the pigskin coat Colin wears—grabbed from the seat of Jack's pickup. The coat is heavy-looking. Rich. At least Jack's not around to see Colin wearing it. He called to tell Diana he made it to Florida. I hope he stays there—forever.

The light wind breaks against my face. It smells of earth, dried leaves and corn. Colin digs the shovel into the dirt. Again. And again. "Colin!" I say. "Stop digging. Please. Stop."

He pauses. Shadows hide his face. His wind-tossed hair looks black. How could I have wanted to touch that hair? Kiss that mouth? "Just stop shoveling, okay? You're making me nervous."

"What are you afraid of, Willo?"

"What do you think?" It's all so obvious, I don't want to talk about it. If he doesn't stop digging, he'll hit Sultan.

"Oh my goodness! Look at that!" Dove points to the sky above our heads. Way up high, ragged clouds race through deep black outer space. They sail across the moon and stars at what seems to be a million miles an hour. It's as if all of heaven has gone crazy.

"If that wind comes to earth, you'll never get your boat back across the creek," Colin says. "You'd better leave. Now."

"Not until we plant our tree." Dove removes the burlap that we've wrapped around the roots. She kneels and sets the tiny roots within the dark hole, huge and gaping. A gust of wind fills her loose jacket. Makes it billow out like wings.

"What a dumb-looking tree," Colin says.

"Then why'd you dig the hole for it?" I say. "Why'd you come out here, anyway?"

"I don't know." Colin's eyes look huge and dark and haunted. The wind blows his hair straight back off his forehead. Blows his coat wide open. His collarbone sticks out, thin and white. I can see his ribs. A scar runs across them. I didn't know he had that scar.

"I love Christmas trees." With one hand, Dove holds ours upright above the gaping hole. With the other, she tries to scoop dirt in around it.

I kneel beside Dove and help her throw in handfuls of moist black dirt. "Christmas trees are beautiful," I say. "They stay green all year long. Their roots are anchored deep in the earth. Their branches reach for heaven. You can decorate them with Christmas balls and lights. You can put presents under them."

"There's a body of a horse beneath this tree," Colin says. "Do you call that a present?"

"No!" I say. "And why'd you have to go and say it?"

"Because it's true. Sultan's body is right beneath your knees. You can't change that. You can't change anything."

"Yes, you can," I say.

"You can't change a single thing." Colin's words are like a shovel, cutting deep.

"We need water." I feel like I'm about to cry. "We can't plant a Christmas tree without water."

Dove grabs a handful of dirt, squeezes it, then lets the dirt fall. "The ground seems moist enough, Willo. The tree should be okay."

"No. Tree roots need water. Lots of water. My mom said so. My mom knew all about Christmas trees." Tears fill my eyes. "Oh, what's the use." I sit back on my heels and I look up at Colin. "We'd need a creek. We'd need a river. We'd need an entire ocean of water to plant this little tree. You're right. It *is* stupid. We can't change anything."

"Yes we can, Willo." Dove's voice sounds full of tears. "All we need is a *little* water." She leans against me, and suddenly, we both are crying.

"Spit," Colin says. His voice sounds funny. It sounds as if it comes from someplace far away and deep. What does he mean—spit?

"Huh?" Dove says.

"You want water? You and Willo want to change things? Then don't cry—spit." Colin kneels beside us and rests his forearms on the loose cold dirt. He spits at tiny roots spread out like a spider's web across the soil. He's crazy. Dove wipes off her tears and grins at me over Colin's back. Suddenly, I'm grinning, too; this is something I can handle.

We spit with Colin. We spit until our mouths and throats are dry. We reach down inside ourselves for whatever we have left and we spit that, too. It may not be enough water, but for the moment, it will do. We pack spit-wet dirt around our tree and it stands by itself, waving soft green branches.

Spit.

Dove sits back on her heels. She looks at Colin. She looks at me. She bows her head and we bow ours. Sounding just like her Grandma Josefa, she prays slowly in Spanish:

> *Se llevó mi voluntad.*
> *Yo le dí mi entendimiento . . .*
> *Me ha dejado la memoria*
> *Para encantar su recuerdo.*

I don't know what the words mean, but they sound sad and beautiful and dreamy. I hope that somewhere, Sultan hears them. Wherever Mom may be, I hope she hears them, too. I imagine her galloping Sultan into heaven's ocean—*God be with you.*

And oh, the wind is roaring now. It roars through nearby cornstalks and trees; it sends an ocean of leaves into our faces. Do the souls of the dead visit us as leaves? They are such beautiful leaves. We laugh as we reach out to hug them. Red ones. Gold ones. Orange ones. Brown. Thousands of them. Millions.

CHAPTER
32

A red leaf is caught in Dove's curly hair, spread out across the pillow next to mine. It's the first thing I see, awakening at seven A.M. My eyes feel gritty; I've had little sleep. Dove, Colin and I kept vigil by Sultan's grave all through the night. Dove sat on one side of Colin. I sat on the other.

We talked and talked while the wind blew leaves all over us. The night grew so dark. But then, this pale light came seeping over the edge of the world and birds began to sing. I said good-bye to Colin. He held me. He kissed me. Now, in my Great-grandmother

Elsie's horsehair bed in Granddad's house, I smell bacon frying.

I climb over Dove, leaving her to sleep a little longer. As I descend the stairs into the living room, I pick up speed. I squarely face the step before the landing I've tried to jump a million times.

Grabbing the balled end of the banister post, I pivot off my left hand. I fly through the air, reaching with my feet for the living room floor. I clear the landing but crash forward onto my hands and knees. I didn't fall backward, though. I'm improving.

"Willo? Are you all right?" Dad stands at the living-room window. Has he been looking at the creek? I hope we tied *The Admiral* up all right.

"I'm fine."

"Come on over here," he says, and my heart leaps into my throat. *Does he know that I snuck out?* He taps a rolled-up sheet of paper against his leg. "That was quite a windstorm we had last night. Look at the creek."

Fog rises off Maiden Creek's dark water. It's covered in leaves. The wind's blown the tide into the creek and high water laps at the top of the dock. Colin was wrong about the wind. It gave no problems to *The Admiral.* That wonderful wind practically blew the old boat back.

Beside me, Dad fidgets, tapping the rolled-up paper against his leg. *Something's coming.* "Did you hear the news?" he says, and then, "No. How could you. I only discovered the fax this morning."

"What is it, Dad?"

"According to this"—he holds up the sheet of paper—"the head of the U.S. Navy has decided to go to bat for the Stealth Intruder. He's meeting with a member of Congress on Monday. He thinks he can convince the government to fork over money to support my project."

"Wow, Dad. That's great news." Why don't I feel happy? "Does this mean you'll be going back to California?"

"For a few weeks."

I gaze past Dad to the creek. Red, gold, orange, yellow and brown leaves float on the beautiful dark water. How can he go away and leave again? How can he leave me?

"It's been a rough year, Willo." Dad reaches out and puts his arm around me. I lean into him. My dad smells good right now. A scrubbed and soapy-smelling clean. He kisses the top of my head. "After this project, I'm still insisting that I work in Baltimore. I'm ready for a change."

"Me, too." I find myself saying, "Want to go sailing for the day? I could crew for you."

"Willojean, Willojean. Sweetest gal I've ever seen," he sings softly. And then he says what I both hoped and feared. "We'll sail tomorrow. Today, you have a horse to show me you know how to ride."

My horse worries at her bit. Sweat darkens her neck. She's as uneasy as I am, making serpentines—snakelike connected loops—across the top end of the field behind the barn. I chose this field to ride in. If I can control Tess here, I can control her anywhere.

Downhill and over to our left, Granddad stands in front of an old hay rake, its rusty tongs clawing at the sky. Dad should be at Granddad's side. The last time I saw him, he was heading for the creek to check on the *Bonnie Prince Charlie*. Tess tosses her head, throwing froth on me. She's holding her head too high. Four months of work for this? I thought she was a forgiving horse.

She jostles me back and forth, jogging nervously toward the shack where Granddad once scalded pigs. Beside him a pile of metal sheets he used to repair the old storage shed blazes in the sun. "Push Tess onto the bit," he calls. "*Use* those boots I bought you."

"Yessir." I sit deep. I use my boots. I pull Tess left. We head across the crest of the hill toward the woods bordering the back end of the field. Tess prances and swishes her tail. I am so tense. *Where's Dad?* Beneath me, Tess feels like she's ready to explode.

"Willo, you're not pushing," Granddad calls.

"Yes I am. It hurts!"

"Do it anyway."

I push hard through the ache. Tess continues to fight me. She seems to think of one thing only—running away. From the bit. From me. The only thing she wants is Toby and he's in the barn. Dove's standing at the barnyard gate. Unlike Dad, Dove's come to watch. "Spit." She mouths that word at me.

When I turn Tess left at the tree line, I stop urging her forward because we're heading downhill now toward the pile of metal sheets and that hay rake. It's easy to imagine arms and legs and hooves getting tangled up in rusty tongs.

"That hay rake could cut us to smithereens," I tell Tess.

"That's it," Granddad says, "talk to her."

I talk to Tess all right. I tell her, "Dad said he'd come out and watch. Where is he? I bet he's at the creek with the *Bonnie Prince Charlie.* But know what, Tess? We just can't let that bother us."

I turn her right and we head back across the field again. Overhead, the sky is filled with white wisps of clouds. Mares' tails, Mom had called them.

My mare prances through a matted clump of grass and her hooves kick up a large dark leaf. The leaf, with no apparent wind to move it, skitters along the ground in front of Tess. *That's strange.*

Tess lowers her head to investigate the leaf. As she does, for the first time since I mounted her today, I feel the weight of Tess's mouth drop into my hands. It seems like a bolt of lightning, connecting her to me.

With my legs and seat, I push Tess gently forward. I close my fingers on the reins and feel her weight through them. Light and easy. On the bit. *She's on the bit.* "You're such a good girl, Tess. Such a good girl. Oh, everything has been so hard."

I release my fingers slightly. Tighten them again. Give and take. Tess responds, slowing to a jog that I can sit to. The leaf teases her; it flutters just ahead of her nose. Tess snorts and the leaf slips through the fence. The dark leaf dances over still and silent piles of brush and disappears into the forest.

"Now you're getting it," Granddad says.

I ask my mare to walk. She seems ready to walk now. She settles into an easy stride. Tess's hooves brush through grass the hay rake cuts through, grabbing at the sky.

As we head uphill again, I squeeze my right leg against Tess; I ask my mare to canter. She breaks into the left lead. She canters slow and easy. I think of a rope, anchored, like a Christmas tree, to something solid. I sit deep. I love the feel of Tess's mouth against the bit. Love the way she feels beneath me—gathered and controlled. We belong together.

I grin. The wind picks up. It blows into my face. A northwest wind. A sailing wind. I bet Dad's gone sailing. The *Bonnie Prince* will heel over until water just about buries its rail—

"You're looking good, Willo," Granddad says. I glance over at him. Dad stands beside my granddad. When did Dad arrive? He watches Tess and me with eyes the color of the Pacific Ocean. As we canter past him, I nod to my commanding officer. He nods back. He smiles and gives the thumbs-up sign.

Sally M. Keehn grew up on her grandfather's farm in Maryland, where she spent her time reading, horseback riding, and exploring. She, like Willojean, fell in love with the first horse she saw, a mare named UpAnchor.

She is the author of two previous novels, *I Am Regina* and *Moon of Two Dark Horses*.

Sally Keehn and her husband live in Allentown, Pennsylvania. They have two daughters.